angels next door

Karen McCombie

PUFFIN

PUFFIN BOOKS

Published by the Penguin Group
Penguin Books Ltd, 80 Strand, London WC2R ORL, England
Penguin Group (USA) Inc., 375 Hudson Street, New York, New York 10014, USA
Penguin Group (Canada), 90 Eglinton Avenue East, Suite 700, Toronto, Ontario, Canada M4P 2Y3
(a division of Pearson Penguin Canada Inc.)
Penguin Ireland, 25 St Stephen's Green, Dublin 2, Ireland (a division of Penguin Books Ltd)
Penguin Group (Australia), 707 Collins Street, Melbourne, Victoria 3008, Australia
(a division of Pearson Australia Group Pty Ltd)
Penguin Books India Pvt Ltd, 11 Community Centre, Panchsheel Park, New Delhi – 110 017, India
Penguin Group (NZ), 67 Apollo Drive, Rosedale, Auckland 0632, New Zealand
(a division of Pearson New Zealand Ltd)
Penguin Books (South Africa) (Pty) Ltd, Block D, Rosebank Office Park,
181 Jan Smuts Avenue, Parktown North, Gauteng 2193, South Africa

Penguin Books Ltd, Registered Offices: 80 Strand, London WC2R ORL, England

puffinbooks.com

First published 2014
001

Text copyright © Karen McCombie, 2014
Chapter illustrations by Madeline Meckiffe
All rights reserved

The moral right of the author and illustrator has been asserted

Set in 13/20pt Baskerville MT Std
Typeset by Jouve (UK), Milton Keynes
Printed in Great Britain by Clays Ltd, St Ives plc

British Library Cataloguing in Publication Data
A CIP catalogue record for this book is available from the British Library

ISBN: 978-0-141-34452-2

www.greenpenguin.co.uk

MIX
Paper from
responsible sources
FSC
www.fsc.org   FSC™ C018179

Penguin Books is committed to a sustainable
future for our business, our readers and our planet.
This book is made from Forest Stewardship
Council™ certified paper.

For Milly, my wee angel . . .

Contents

Before everything changed . . .   1

How to be only me   10

Please, Miss . . . *help*!   24

The recipe for Awkward Shy Jelly   35

Hello, trouble   54

Do I *look* like a dog?   79

The small thing that blew my mind   92

Come inside . . .?   113

Sort ofs and shocks   132

Unless . . . what if?   141

They like me, they like me not   154

Floating, flying, free   164

The opposite of wonderful   173

With a rustle and a flutter   196

After everything changed . . .   217

Acknowledgements   226

Before everything changed . . .

I have the *strangest* feeling.

If I was at home I'd think Dot was standing over me, trying not to giggle while she sprinkled glitter on my face, after telling me to lie down and shut my eyes.

But I'm not at home.

Dot's nowhere in sight – she's gone for a playdate this afternoon with her little friend Coco.

And as I brush my face I realize there's nothing on it – no glitter, no nothing – except warm September sunshine.

So what was that all about? Who knows? Though

what I *do* know is that I'm sometimes very good at imagining things . . . I give myself a small shuddery shake and get back to what's real.

And right now I'm in my favourite place, with my favourite person: my forever friend, Tia.

Me and Tia are doing what we do best.

Lying on our backs at the top of Folly Hill, right by the Angel.

Feeling the soft green grass on our bare legs and arms.

Staring at the blue, blue sky and the skimming white clouds.

Talking about everything.

Talking about nothing.

It's been the same since we were little kids of six. Back then we used to curtsy to the stone angel, perched prettily on her plinth. Obviously, we don't do that any more. I mean, as Tia once pointed out, what's cute when you're six can look slightly *insane* to passing strollers and dog-walkers when you're nearly twelve.

And, funnily enough, today we're talking about birthdays, since mine isn't all that far away.

'Hey, *I* know what I want!' I say, having thought about it *right* before I felt that non-existent sprinkle of glitter.

Me and Tia – up till now our heads have been touching, the fingertips of my right hand brushing the fingertips of Tia's left hand. But as I wait for my friend to respond I flip round on to my tummy, wriggle my camera out from my coat pocket and point it at Tia.

SNAP!

'Yeah? What's that, then?' Tia mutters.

Her eyes are closed against the late-afternoon light, spiralling dark curls spread round her head like a halo. She'll have heard the click of the camera, but it won't have bothered her; she's used to me and my habit of taking pictures of her, of us, of what we get up to. I only use the camera when it's just me and Tia – it was an eighth-birthday present from Dad and is now *way* too pink and plastic and rubbish to be seen out in public.

'You want to know? Well, I'm going to tell you!' I say excitably.

By the way, I'm only ever excitable with Tia. In my old school reports from Beechwood Primary, they always wrote that I was shy and never very good at joining in. We haven't had any reports from Hillcrest Academy yet – we're only a couple of weeks into our very first term – but I'm betting the teachers there will say *exactly* the same thing.

And I guess those descriptions of me are pretty accurate. I know that's how people see me, and I don't mean just teachers. It's the other kids as well, and sometimes my family too.

Not Dot, though. Dot – like Tia – sees a different side of me.

Tia knows me inside out, upside down, cos she's been my best friend since we were six, when she bounced into school with a smile a mile wide, directed – amazingly – straight at shy-girl me.

And *Dot* . . . well, she's five, and five-year-olds don't let you get away with not joining in, whether it's playing I Spy or having a how-many-Hula-Hoops-can-you-cram-in-your-mouth-at-once competition (sixteen, if you were wondering).

'OK, so *here's* what I want for my birthday,' I continue brightly. One hand lets go of the camera, and I begin to reel off my pressie wish list on my fingers. 'Eyes the colour of the sky . . .'

The corners of Tia's mouth twitch in a smile.

'Hair as sheeny and shiny as silk, and long, long, *long* – all the way to my waist.'

Tia smiles some more, but her eyes are still shut.

'Skin smooth as the white marble of the Angel.' Scratching the couple of spots that have pinged on to my chin in the last week, I gaze up at the Angel. When I was little I used to pretend she was my mother, switched to stone by an evil witch. Ha!

SNAP! goes the camera, capturing the pale stone against the pastel sky.

'Oh, and maybe a birthmark in the shape of a heart,' I finish with.

One of Tia's eyes flips open at that. 'Why?' she asks, squinting at me and grinning at my ramblings.

'Just because it would be nice if I could magically *change* on my twelfth birthday,' I say, flopping back on to the grass. 'I'm a bit fed up of being me.'

SNAP! to the sky, and the scudding clouds.

'Don't be silly,' Tia mumbles, but not unkindly. Though it's easy for *her* to say.

Out of the two of us, she's the Confident One, the Gorgeous One. If I had to describe what she looks like, I'd use delicious words. Hair the colour of treacle; skin the colour of caramel; eyes shiny as golden syrup.

I'm the Quiet One. Ask anyone to describe what *I* look like and they'd probably say, 'Who?'

With my pale, mousy hair and eyes the colour of a muddy puddle, I'm so ordinary I'm practically invisible . . .

It would be nice to be as interesting, as pretty, as

3-D as Tia. But I have the next best thing, I suppose. I have *Tia*. Always there, always looking out for me.

'At least my actual birthday will be fun,' I natter on, my eyes on the skipping drifts of clouds in the viewfinder. 'I can't believe we're going on the school trip on the same day. How lucky is that?'

Tia says nothing. She's daydreaming, imagining us at the Wildwoods Theme Park, trying to decide which of the amazing rides we'll go on, I bet.

'So are you planning to sing "Happy Birthday" to me from the top of the Sky Coaster?' I suggest. 'Or will you be too busy screaming?'

I hear Tia make a noise like a sigh. A happy sigh, I guess. A sigh that probably says, *I can't wait . . .*

'Maybe I could take a cake along! Wouldn't that be funny?' I chit-chat. 'Mrs Sharma could look after it; it's not as if she'll be able to go on any of the rides, is it?'

Our form teacher was already pretty pregnant when we were introduced to her at the start of term. In another few weeks, she'll be *huge*.

Tia doesn't say anything to that.

Which suddenly seems a bit odd.

My dad calls her Little Miss Chatterbox. Her own dad's nickname for her is Bunny, since she never stops rabbiting on. And Mrs Sharma's *already* had to have a word with her about yakking in class.

Y'know, Tia not jumping in with a comment, a question, a joke . . . it doesn't seem *right*, somehow.

'So what do you think?' I press her. 'Should I write a list of *Things I Want to Change*? I could leave it under my pillow the night before my birthday, like you do with the tooth fairy. And maybe, *magically* –'

'The thing is, Riley,' Tia suddenly interrupts, '*everything's* going to change . . .'

For a long, silent second, it's like the whole world's stalled, as still as the stone angel behind us.

I have no idea what my best friend means. All I know is that it feels like someone has just placed a granite block on my chest. It's heavy, it hurts and it's made of pure dread.

Everything's going to change, I repeat to myself silently.

The dread catches hold of me again and I'm too scared to ask Tia what she means. What if she tells me something I don't want to hear? Instead, I stare up at the wispy white clouds trailing across the blue sky, my camera hiding eyes stinging so much it's as if *real* glitter had landed in them.

SNAP!

What exactly is fate blowing my way? I fret to myself.

I suddenly *badly* want to change my stupid wish.

Can everything stay the same?

Please?

I squeeze my eyes tight shut and try listening out for a voice – a certain far-away, comforting voice – that might make everything all right.

Instead, Tia starts talking again. 'It's like this, Riley,' she begins.

And, as she begins, my world ends . . .

How to be only me

'*It's going to be all right, Riley.*'

No, it's not.

My eyes are squeezed tight shut.

So tight I can see spangles of bright light dancing against the darkness of my eyelids.

The eyes-squeezed-tight thing – I guess I do it whenever I'm stressed or angry. (Like now.)

And I really, really shouldn't, cos *that's* when I seem to hear her voice . . . soft and kind, but far-away and scratchy too, as if I'm listening to a badly tuned-in radio in a different room.

'*It's going to be all right, Riley.*'

Ping! My eyes open wide. Not because I've relaxed, suddenly believing what the breathy, dreamy voice has just told me. Oh no. It's because I'm reminding myself that it's dumb to take advice from someone:

a) who isn't really there, and
b) who's actually dead.

(Sorry, Mum, but it's true . . .)

And so it's back to the watery lemon of this bright October morning and the view that I hate.

I'm not talking about Chestnut Crescent, where I live with Dad, Hazel and Dot. I mean, it's just an ordinary street with a bunch of ordinary modern houses in it. Some small-ish trees, cars in drives, chucked-aside kids' scooters.

I'm not talking about Folly Hill, rising up behind our sleepy suburb, the Angel at the top, watching us all with her carved, kind eyes.

And I'm not talking about the view of the town

stretching out in front of us like a patchwork map of streets and buildings.

I'm talking about the view from my front steps. Our crescent, just like you'd expect from the name, curves round. And that means that from where I'm sitting (top step) I get a clear, nearly right-angle view of the house next door.

It's the house next door that I'm staring at, hating it.

Hating it because it's empty.

Hating it because its two large front windows – minus curtains – look like sad, empty eyes on either side of the cheery cherry-red front door.

Hating it, because Tia doesn't live at number thirty-three any more. Which means nothing can ever be all right again, no matter what those half-heard murmurs try to tell me.

'Riley! RILEY!'

The high voice buzzes like a mosquito. I try to block it out, hunching lower on the cool front step, hoping Dot doesn't realize I'm still out here.

'Riley! RILEY! *RILEY!!*' My sort-of-stepsister's voice shrills closer as skippetty footsteps kerplunk along the hallway behind me.

Sigh . . .

I wrap my fingers round the bottom of the slightly ajar front door and try to pull it closed to hide myself, but it's too late.

'Riley!' yelps Dot, yanking the door fully open and spilling out on to the top step. 'Look! *Look*, Riley! LOOK!!'

'Uh-huh,' I say vaguely as she twirls in a whirl of pleated grey school skirt and nearly treads on my fingers with her shiny school shoes.

Hanging out with Dot can be fun but I definitely don't have the patience for her today. I've been crying so much that my head is thumping and my heart is splitting, in that order. I don't know *how* I'll get the energy to hoist myself up and gather my school stuff together.

And I certainly don't have the energy for one over-excited five-year-old.

'But *look*! Riley – see? SEE what happens when I do *this*?' Dot giggles, grabbing the bottom edges of her cardigan and holding them up behind her. 'It makes it seem like I've got *wings*, doesn't it? HA, HA, HA!' With that, she gallops around, flapping madly.

I sigh to myself again, wondering if there's anything wrong with Dot's eyesight. Hasn't she noticed how deeply navy blue I am? Didn't she see Dad hugging me before he left, while I sobbed a large wet patch on his neatly ironed work shirt? ('Hey, I know it's tough, Riley,' he'd said, trying to soothe me, 'but it won't always hurt this badly, I promise.' Yeah, *right*.)

Though maybe Dot *isn't* being thoughtless. Maybe she's trying to distract me, to take my mind off the fact that my best – my forever and always – friend has finally, really and truly moved away.

Moved far away, miles away, half a world away, to New Zealand.

Home of fault-lines and earthquakes and seismic

strangeness, as I pointed out to Tia when she first broke the news – that sunny September afternoon on Folly Hill only a few weeks ago – that her family was emigrating.

'*And* where they filmed *Lord of the Rings*, don't forget,' she'd said, laughing at me and showing off the cute gap in her front teeth. 'Hey, I've got to show you the latest photo of the house Mum and Dad want to check out. Get this – the swimming pool is kidney-shaped!'

I've always loved Tia's confidence and enthusiasm. Whenever I've been too scared or too shy to do something, she's been right beside me, telling me why I *can* jump from the top board, why I *am* better than the bullies at school, why it *is* a good idea to try on the fun wigs in Claire's Accessories and take pictures of each other, even if people are staring at us like we're mad. For as long as I can remember, just because she is who she is, Tia's made me braver than I could ever be on my own. But, for some reason, her enthusiasm for the stupid kidney-shaped swimming pool really *hurt*. Like some dumb swimming pool would make up for leaving me behind . . .

Of course, Tia won't be swimming in her fancy kidney-shaped pool *quite* yet. She won't even be three quarters of the way to the *airport*. She and her parents only drove off ten minutes ago, following the giant lumbering removal van.

As she waved madly out of the back window, I saw the glint of a tear on her light-brown cheek. (OK, so if I didn't know it already, that proved the stupid swimming pool didn't really mean that much to her.)

All Tia will have seen of *me* was a big pink marshmallow face, swollen and soggy from sobbing. What a great memory to carry away with her . . .

Blue, blue, navy blue.

Life from now on is going to be empty and lonely and I might as well trudge back upstairs to my bedroom, slither under my squashy duvet and never bother coming out . . .

'Dot – I already told you to stop doing that. You'll stretch your new cardigan!' comes Hazel's voice now. It's slightly muffled as my dad's girlfriend busily stuffs her white nurses' shoes in her bag and wriggles herself into her jacket, ready for her shift at the hospital. 'We have to go, or we're going to be late. Say bye to Alastair quickly . . .'

Dot gives a squeak and skittles back inside to pat her pet, while I use the cuff of my jumper to rub away some sparkly fingerprints Dot's left on the door (or she'll get into trouble for mucking around with glitter too).

'Hey, here's your gym kit, Riley,' Hazel says, passing me a green nylon bag as well as my school backpack.

My thanks are drowned out as Dot clatters and sing-songs along the hall, her pet patted and her lunchbox grabbed.

'So new term, new start, eh, Riley?' Hazel says in that matter-of-fact nurse voice that she probably uses on her patients. Her patients and *me*. (Never

Dad or Dot, funnily enough – they get the sugar-coated voice.)

Well, *technically*, it's the second half of the autumn term, but I don't bother saying so, since I'm pretty sure that was a rhetorical question. Hazel's busily rummaging in her bag for her keys, as if her mind's already switched off from me and the least fun school holidays ever.

I mean, I usually *love* being off school, spending long, lazy days hanging out in Tia's super-cool bedroom in the loft. We'd lounge in front of her very own telly, play the Wii, dance along to music vids on MTV, with the metallic-pink patterned wallpaper making us feel like we were in a club. But this half-term week all I did was help Tia pack her stuff into boxes, as if I was helping her to leave me.

'See you later,' I mumble, pushing myself upright and leaving Hazel and Dot to bustle their way out of the house and into the car.

Hoisting my bag and gym kit over my shoulder, I begin to follow the steady stream of black-blazered kids laughing, joking, trudging or fooling their way along the road together to our big, blocky secondary school that's just round the corner and across the manic whizz of Meadow Lane.

'Ah, such a *peaceful* country road!' I remember Tia once saying with a knowing smirk. She took a deep breath of non-existent flowers and hedgerows as we stood at the teeming junction, cars and lorries hurtling by in a fug of fumes.

I smile a wobbly smile at the memory, and then the tears prick my eyes again as I realize with a punch to the chest that there'll be no more strolls to school with chats and giggles and hey-listen-to-this gossip. I'll only have a Tia-shaped space for company.

The trouble is I can't fit in with anyone in my class. The boys, no way. They're split into either the football or the game-geek gangs, and none of them bothers with girls unless it's to laugh at them. As for the girls, well, *all* of them came from different primary schools to me and Tia, and although they're pretty nice, they were already in their tight little cliques when they arrived at Hillcrest and have stayed that way. Of course, *one* clique I have no interest in *ever* joining is Lauren Mayhew's. She and Joelle Hunter and Nancy Adams like to think they're royalty in Class Y7C – ruling with sarky digs and sharp words – though me and Tia have done a pretty good job of staying under their radar so far.

But, with no bright, shining, ever-smiling Tia to hide behind, will it stay that way?

You know, it would be *so* much easier if I could just turn invisible. The superpower of invisibility; *that's* what I should ask for, for my birthday . . .

Thwack!!

Half a second ago I'd been vaguely aware of the general noise of boys right behind me, playfighting, goofing around, whatever.

Now someone – or maybe *more* than one someone – has stupidly staggered into me and I'm stumbling, tumbling sideways, the pavement lunging towards me alarmingly fast.

'Oww . . .' I groan as pain jars viciously through the elbow I've landed on.

So much for invisibility. As I wince and try to catch my breath, I find myself staring up at a pack of jeering Cheshire cats.

'She's Tia's mate, isn't she?' says a boy I vaguely recognize from the year above me.

'What – is Tia that really pretty one?' says another voice.

'Yeah,' says the first boy. 'But shame . . . she's leaving. She's going to Australia or somewhere.'

Tia isn't leaving; she's left.

It's New Zealand; not Australia.

But I don't come out with either of those things, because pain and embarrassment have tightened my throat so I can't make a sound.

Hey, boys, don't anybody rush to help me up, I complain silently to myself instead.

Maybe a second too soon as it happens.

'Hand?' says someone, reaching down to me.

From my viewpoint – i.e. the pavement – I see a

wide grin, with dimples either side, along with spiky dark hair and a fan of freckles across the nose and cheeks. All of that together means one thing, or one person in particular, JD, from *our* year, from Y7A to be exact. He's this boy who had a bit of a crush on Tia all last half-term. She nicknamed him JD – short for Join the Dots cos of the freckles – but his real name's Woody. Sometimes he'd catch up with us on the way to school or home and tell us endless jokes. That's till Tia blanked him enough times that he got the message and slunk off. I felt kind of bad about it, but Tia was firm. 'Look, if I act friendly we'll *never* get rid of him, Riley!' she'd pointed out.

Wincing, I blink up at his smiling face. I *want* to trust him (I want to get up off this pavement), but what if that's a smile *at* me, not *for* me? What if JD pulls his hand away as soon as I reach for it, as an added bit of entertainment for his Year 8 buddies – *and* to get back at me for Tia's non-interest?

'I'm fine,' I lie, wishing JD would stop staring at me and mooch off with his mates instead.

'If you're fine, then I'm Robert Pattinson,' he jokes in his usual lame way.

Actually, that is almost funny. But, then again, is he laughing *at* me?

If that's what's going on, then there's no *way* I'm taking that hand he's still holding out.

'Looks like you're wasting your time, mate,' one of the Year 8s says, sounding bored of the situation now.

'Yeah, come on,' says another, slapping JD's shoulder. 'If she doesn't want your help, then leave her alone.'

And so that's what JD does – leaves me alone – and trundles away with the rest of the gang of lads.

But that's the problem, I admit to myself as I lie here on the cold, hard ground.

It doesn't matter about those words I imagine my mum saying. It's *never* going to be all right. Cos it's only ever been Tia and Riley, Riley and Tia.

I just don't *know* how to be alone.

How do I be only me?

Please, Miss . . . help!

I hadn't planned on having a very good day today, but it seems to be getting more awful by the minute.

Tugging at the bottom of my top, I squeak the changing-room door open, *just about* hearing the general chit-chatter of the class above the sound of my thumping heart.

'Ah, Riley!' booms Mrs Zucker. 'At last, you've *finally* joined . . .'

It's not just our PE teacher's voice that trails off. The chit-chatter has died away, and there's a stupefied silence in its place.

'Pffft!' The first snort comes from Lauren Mayhew. No surprises there.

'Fnarrrrr-a-hur-a-hur!'

I don't know who *that* was – one or other of the boys. But it doesn't exactly matter, not when there's an immediate wall of laughter so loud it's slamming into me, hard as bricks.

Great. Everyone's finding me completely *hilarious* this morning, thanks to Hazel putting the wrong newly washed gym kit in the wrong bag. Which means at *some* point today, Dot will be giggling her way through star-jumps and trampette bounces at her primary school while wearing an age-twelve Hillcrest Academy white polo shirt.

With trembling hands, I tug again at the way, *way* too short hem of the age-five-to-seven Peppa Pig top I'm squashed into. I lower my eyes from the twenty-six classmates who are roaring like I'm the funniest thing since a *You've Been Framed* clip of someone cycling into a wall. I immediately regret it, since it means my gaze is now on the stray and slightly grubby pair of XL boys' football shorts that Mrs Zucker found for me in the store-room.

'Actually, no . . . that's not going to work, is it?' Mrs Zucker says, walking over to me and frowning. 'I thought we could get away with you wearing that top, since you girls tend to like your clothes tight, but . . .'

She doesn't need to finish the sentence. The top is so small the sleeves are cutting off the circulation at the top of my arms and a distorted Peppa Pig is stretched so fiercely she's flattening what little chest I've got.

'Listen, Riley,' says Mrs Zucker, raising her voice to be heard above the continuing echoing cackles. 'Go and have a look in the lost-property box beside Mr Bradley's office. See if there's anything you can grab out of there instead.'

A bit of pride, maybe, since I've lost all mine? I think bleakly as I pad out of the gym into the cool, empty corridor.

The annexe is thankfully quiet – there's nothing

here except the gym, the changing rooms and the site manager's office, so there's no chance of any passing students catching a glimpse of my joke gym kit.

I take a deep, juddering breath, put my forehead against the pale green wall and squeeze my eyes tight closed, willing myself not to cry.

'All right, Riley?' a gentle voice suddenly asks me.

My head tilts up and I see Mrs Sharma, my form teacher, coming out of the site manager's office. She's smiley, small and very, *very* round.

'I've just left a note on Mr Bradley's desk about that tap that's leaking in my classroom,' she says, yanking the stiff office door shut with one hand while the other rests on the ledge of her can't-miss-it baby bump. 'For some reason his office phone isn't working, so I had to walk *all* the way along here, which isn't easy in *my* condition! Hey – are you OK, Riley?' she says, clearly spotting something's up.

That's it.

That's all I need – someone being nice makes me well up again.

'Here, come on into the office . . . Mr Bradley's going to have a first-aid kit somewhere in here, and we can have a chat,' says Mrs Sharma, wrestling the stiff door open, helped by a determined bang of her hip.

Lovely Mrs Sharma. It was my grazed elbow – from my fall on the way to school this morning – that she'd noticed at first. But she's pretty smart and kind and I think she's figured out that it's not the only thing troubling me.

Mrs Sharma shoves the door closed behind us, leads me to a chair and bundles a tissue into my hand, just in case.

'Ah, here we are! Now let's see if we can find you a plaster,' she says, crouching down beside a small wooden cabinet with a green cross on it. 'And while I fix you up maybe we can have a chat about anything else going on with you, Riley?'

Oh yeah? And what can I tell her exactly?

Please, Miss, I got thwacked to the ground by a bunch of boys.

Please, Miss, I've just been humiliated in front of my entire class.

Please, Miss, today I lost my best friend forever, *forever*.

Please, Miss, I don't think this day could get any worse . . .

'It's T-T-Ti–' I hiccup as tears threaten again. But, before I can splutter out my friend's name, Mrs Sharma speaks. Sort of.

'Ohhhh . . .!'

Huh?

My form teacher has been crouched down in the same position for a while now. I can see she has a plaster in her hand – so why isn't she getting up? And why did she just say 'Ohhhh . . .!' in that funny way?

'Huh-*nnnnnggg* . . .'

Huh-*nnnnnggg*?

I don't like the sound of that.

And I don't like the way she's just leaned forward, dropping on to her knees and flopping her head on to the top of the first-aid cabinet.

'Mrs Sharma?!' I say in alarm.

Nothing.

I hurtle out of my chair and tentatively go to touch her on the arm, scared that she might have just gone and *died* on me.

'Riley . . .' Mrs Sharma groans, making me jump.

Of course I'm pleased she's not dead (that would REALLY make this day immensely worse), but I'm a bit freaked out that she's said my name in a growly voice like she's *possessed* or something.

'The baby . . . I think it's coming. You need to get help.'

Before she's finished the word 'help', I'm already picking up the phone on the desk, ready to ring the school office.

Big problem: I hear the dead tone and remember Mrs Sharma saying she hadn't been able to get through to Mr Bradley's phone.

I've no sooner clattered the phone back down on the desk than in one bound of my flippy-flappy XL shorts I'm clutching the doorknob – the very stiff doorknob that Mrs Sharma was struggling with a minute ago – but it's got absolutely no intention of turning.

'Excuse me, but do you have your mobile on you, Mrs Sharma?' I say, feeling beads of sweat break out on my forehead as I struggle with the jammed door.

'No . . .' she wheezes weakly, caught up in her own struggle. ''S in my locker, in – *huh!* – the staffroom.'

We're both gasping, for our own different reasons. This isn't good.

You know, I hate the endless TV medical dramas that Hazel makes us watch (so she can criticize them when a nurse bandages someone wrongly, or snogs a doctor behind a pile of cardboard bedpans), but *something* from those telly programmes must have seeped into my head.

'Your breathing . . . you've got to do quick little pants, Mrs Sharma,' I tell her, hoping I sound like I know what I'm talking about. 'Those'll help you get through the pain and keep calm.'

At the word 'calm', the doorknob comes away in my hand and clatters on to the floor.

That's when I lose it.

'HELP!' I yell, slamming my hands on the glass. 'SOMEBODY HELP US!!!'

My yells will be heard by absolutely no one, obviously, since the corridor is empty and the thundering roar of my class as they cheer each other round the timed circuit in the gym would drown me out anyway.

'HEEEEELLLLLPPPPP!!!' I yell at the top of my voice and hammer the glass till it vibrates, just cos I don't know what else to do.

With my eyes scrunched tight, the white dots swirl, and I can hear it – the soothing voice – above my own stressed-out yell.

'*It'll be all right, Riley.*'

The voice: it doesn't sound as if it's in my head any more.

This is weird, seriously weird. It sounds faint and buzzy, as if it's coming from the useless out-of-order phone I chucked on the table a second ago . . .

At the same time a breeze that smells of cut grass and summer skies spins round me, cooling my forehead, sure as a cold, damp cloth.

I open my eyes wide, my heart thundering even faster.

I'm imagining a voice on a broken phone? And a welcome breeze in a windowless box-room-of-an-office?

OK, so I'm flipping out here, but I've *got* to pull myself together, for Mrs Sharma's sake, as well as my own. Opening my mouth, I yell desperately for help again – and find myself staring face to startled face with someone on the other side of the glass door panel.

Mr Bradley the site manager is carrying a cup of coffee and a large screwdriver.

He thought he was coming back to his quiet tucked-away office to fix a bad-tempered doorknob and instead has found it's turned into a combined maternity ward and madhouse.

But thankfully – by the magic of a stiff-but-working knob on the *outside* of the door – Mr Bradley is in the room in a split-second and instantly assessing the mayhem, while I kneel down by a wincing, panting-by-order Mrs Sharma.

'Ambulance, please!' our site manager barks into the mobile he's just pulled out of his back pocket.

'Aaaarghhh!' howls Mrs Sharma as a contraction grips her, and in turn she grips hard – *really* hard – at my hair.

Biting my lip to stop myself crying out, I wonder if today can get any more bizarre.

And then Mrs Sharma unclenches her fist, and a handful of my mousy-brown hair lands on my too-tight Peppa Pig T-shirt.

Well, I guess there's my answer . . .

The recipe for Awkward Shy Jelly

My sort-of-stepsister has an impressive selection of pyjamas, and likes to get in character depending on which set she's wearing.

In her floaty fairy nightie, she'll tiptoe and flap around the house. In her PJs with the glittery pony on the front, she'll canter and whinny (quite annoying when you're trying to do your homework). And in her tiger all-in-one? Well, prepare to be pounced on.

Right now, Dot's chosen to put on the fairy nightie, which she's accessorized with a sparkly plastic wand. She's also insisted on having her bedtime story with me, in my room, at 4.30 p.m., because she feels like it. And I said fine, why not, since:

a) I'm always kind of charmed by Dot's randomness, and
b) it sounded like a lot more fun than the geography homework I was meant to be doing.

'*Big Duck quacked to Little Duck, "I love you!"*' I read aloud, while pushing the wand away so it doesn't poke me in the eye.

Apart from one lethal wand-waving arm, Dot is snuggled under my duvet, not listening to a word I'm saying, I'm pretty sure.

I try a test. '*And then Little Duck quacked to Big Duck, "I love* YOU *as much as porridge!"*'

Not a comment, not a twitch. Dot knows this book inside out, and knows there's nothing about porridge in there (just like I know porridge makes Dot *gag*).

'*And Big Duck quacked to Little Duck, "I love you better than snot!"*'

Still nothing. Nothing except the sense that I'm being stared at, hard.

'*Then Little Duck took out a really big gun and –*'

'Does it hurt?' Dot interrupts.

I look round and see her gazing at me with her owlish brown eyes. 'You mean this?' I ask, holding up the elbow which now has a padded dressing on it, thanks to Hazel. 'Or *this*?'

I point to the pound-coin-sized bald patch on the side of my head, where Mrs Sharma hauled the chunk of hair out.

'No, not *them*. I mean having a baby,' says Dot, gently pressing a fingertip to the hairless spot.

'Um, a little, I guess,' I reply, thinking about the total *agony* Mrs Sharma was in as the ambulance team came to her rescue.

Dot is *completely* blown away by what happened today. She hasn't shut up since she found out. ('I can't believe you borned a baby, Riley!' 'Dot, I didn't "born" a baby. I didn't even really help that much.' 'Was it scary seeing the baby come out?' 'I *told* you: the ambulance lady helped Mrs Sharma have her baby girl. I wasn't allowed to stay in the office.' 'But did you see it coming out just a bit?' 'No.' 'Even just a *little* bit?' 'No!')

Once Dot climbed into (my) bed I thought she'd finally run out of questions, but obviously not.

'*I'm* never going to have any babies, *ever*,' says Dot with a shudder. 'I was telling Mummy that when I'm as old as her I'm going to get *puppies*, and they can play with Alastair!'

I immediately picture the dog basket in the hall downstairs, which contains a tartan blankie, an unchewed chew toy, a big stick and no dog. That's because Dot's darling pet happens to be made of wood.

Yes, *wood*.

Alastair is a hunk of light-as-air driftwood that we found on Whitsea beach back in the summer holidays. It had a whole bunch of knobbles on it that *sort* of looked like legs and ears and a tail if you squinted at it funny. Dot had cooed and cuddled it the whole car journey home, so back at the house I stuck on some googly eyes and drew a nose and sticky-out tongue in black marker pen. She was so thrilled that she saved up her pocket money to buy 'Alastair' a collar and lead and all the other doggy essentials.

'Will you get a prize?' Dot interrupts my thoughts.

'What do you mean, a "prize"?' I frown.

'Like a medal, for helping born your teacher's baby!'

'Dot, I *didn't* help Mrs Sharma give birth!' I tell her yet again.

I wish she'd give up on the whole baby drama; I've had enough of it now. This morning everybody piled out of the gym when they got wind of the ambulance parked outside. Then they crowded round me and my flappy shorts, firing question after question. (All except Lauren, Joelle and Nancy, who hung back and whispered behind their hands, cos that's their style.)

It went on the whole day, with kids I hardly knew coming up and quizzing me, or pointing at me from a distance. Brave, confident Tia Adjaye would have been able to handle all the staring and the gossiping, but not wimpy lip-'n'-nail-biting Riley Roberts.

If you want the recipe for Awkward Shy Jelly, it's this: take me, add lots of unwanted attention and pour out in the shape of a girl. Then watch it wobble . . .

'Do you miss her?' Dot blurts.

'Mrs Sharma?' I ask in surprise, though I don't know why I'm surprised. Dot's conversations tend to jump around as much as she does.

'No!' laughs Dot as if *I'm* the crazy one in this glued-together family of ours.

'Do you mean Tia, then?'

'No!' Dot giggles. 'I mean your mummy!'

I go cold and hot and shivery and very probably pink.

We don't speak about my mum in our family.

At least Dad never speaks about her and I never ask.

It's not because of Hazel; he didn't speak about Mum *way* before they got together. Way before as in hardly *ever*. I mean, he used to answer simple questions when I was young, but always looked so heartbroken that I felt – even as a little kid – that I was hurting him with her memory.

So all I have is my single precious photo, tucked away at the back of my knicker drawer.

That, and a voice I imagine in my head whenever I squeeze my eyes tight shut.

'Dot, why are you asking about my mum?' I say, confused as well as a bit rattled.

'Because she borned you.'

OK, so Dot is *still* obsessed with today's topic of babies.

'Yes, well, my mum died when I was only a few months old, so I don't remember her.'

'But '

'Right, that's it for today,' I cut her off in a friendly but firm way. 'I've got homework to do and I'm sure there's fairy dust to be sprinkled somewhere!'

Perhaps I shouldn't have said that last part – Dot is banned from going within a kilometre of glitter after the incident with the shampoo bottle last week ('I thought it would be nice if we all had sparkly hair!') and she's obviously got an illegal stash of it somewhere, going by the silvery fingerprints on the front door this morning.

But Dot's head is so full of fluff and babies that I don't think she's paying attention to me anyway. I toss the duvet aside so she can flitter and flutter her way out of my room – but it seems that she's not ready to leave *quite* yet.

'You know, it's all right to miss your mummy, Riley,' she says, turning back to me and wrapping her skinny arms round my neck. 'I miss my daddy too.'

Dot's dad, Charlie, lives four streets away and she sees him for tea twice a week and goes to stay with him on alternate weekends. It's not *quite* the same thing.

'Thanks, Dot,' I say anyway, giving her a kiss on the top of her head.

With that, she bounces off the bed and goes skipping and wand-wafting away – then stops *again*, just outside in the corridor this time.

'Hey, Riley – Coco says that angels are coming to live next door!'

Dot's friend Coco thinks ice cream is made of snow and that a small dragon lives in an electricity substation at the end of Chestnut Crescent. I can't say I'd believe everything she has to say. Or *anything*, really.

'That's nice,' I reply, walking over and gently closing the door on her.

I can hear her sing-songing in her happily out-of-tune way and find myself facing my pinboard on the opposite wall. Strolling over, I study the photos stuck on it, all taken on my chunky kiddie camera. Tia's face smiles out at me most, with Dot's coming a close second, then Dad's. (None of Hazel. She *does* smile, just not usually in my direction. Which is why I haven't turned the pink plastic camera in *her* direction too often.)

Look: there's me and Tia with those funny Claire's Accessories wigs on; me and Tia doing useless cartwheels up on Folly Hill; me and Tia dressed as Thing 1 and Thing 2 for World Book Day in Year 5.

But all of a sudden there's one particular photo I want to look at.

One that I haven't seen in a really long time.

One that I didn't take.

I take a sideways step and open my knicker drawer.

Tucked right at the back – under an untidy jumble of pants – is the small plastic folder.

I pull it out, un-pop the popper and let her photo fall out into my hand.

Mum.

She's standing with her arms spread wide, her strawberry-blonde hair blowing and tangly in the breeze. A blissed-out expression on her face, her eyes on the blue sky above. Her bare feet on green grass, her flowery dress fluttering, except where it's covering a big bump (hey, I'd forgotten I was in this picture, in a way!).

I prop the photo up against the mirror on top of my chest of drawers and try to copy Mum's pose.

Turning slightly side on towards the window, I fling my arms back and tilt my face up, but it's no good. I don't feel blissed-out. And I'm not on a summery hilltop; I'm in my lilac-walled bedroom, which can look a little grey and gloomy at this time of day, when the late-afternoon sun's on the other side of the house.

Ping!

Two thoughts suddenly trip into my mind at the same time.

The first is that the hilltop Mum is standing on *has* to be Folly Hill. (I can see a corner of the Angel's plinth at the edge of the photo.) Why haven't I noticed that before?

The second is that it's *exactly* where I want to be right now . . .

'Riley?' Hazel calls out as I thunder down the stairs, grabbing my jacket. 'Where are you going?'

'Up to the Angel! Back in time for tea!' I call to her, heading out of the door.

'But –'

I'm almost always pretty polite to Hazel, but my head is so full that I pretend I haven't heard her 'but' and let the door bang shut behind me.

Following the cut-through paths that link the neighbouring streets, scrunching up the flint path through the grass, it takes me less than five minutes to find myself, breathless, by the Angel.

I throw my arms out wide – like Mum's in the photo – and breathe in the cool air.

It's funny to think that twelve and a bit years ago Mum must have gazed at more or less this exact same view. (Funny, weird . . . and a little bit sad too.)

There's the sprawl of roads I've just run through, and the town beyond.

To the left I can see the towering concrete lump of our school, named after Hillcrest House, the big manor that used to be here. Imagine, a hundred years or so ago, this whole area was just farmland, cows and chestnut trees. Of course, all that's left of the Hillcrest estate is the Angel Folly, built by some rich owner way, way back in Victorian times.

Straight down the hill I can pick out Tia's house really clearly. It's got one of the last of the grand old chestnuts in the garden. When we were younger we'd climb in the branches, sitting there for hours in our own private leafy world.

Oh.

Now I can see a figure coming up the hill towards me, a figure that's *very* familiar. Tall, greying brown hair, suede jacket, jeans – and a huge smile, beaming my way.

Self-consciously I drop my widespread arms and sit on the ground, feeling like I might somehow have done something wrong, just by *thinking* about Mum. Dad is so warm and wonderful, but, like I say, that's a subject that's definitely out of bounds, guaranteed to turn him sad and silent in an instant.

'Dad?' I call out to him as he strides closer. 'Why are you here?'

'I finished work early and was just driving up to the house when I saw you,' he says, flopping down beside me. 'Hazel said you'd come up here, so I thought I'd join you.'

Owning the print shop means Dad can leave one or other of the members of staff in charge and come home when he likes. It means he often picks Dot up from primary school, same as he did with me when I was younger. It means he can surprise me by coming to hang out on the hill, just me and him.

Since Hazel and Dot moved in at the end of last year 'just me and him' doesn't happen very often, so this feels unexpected and nice. I try to shake off the guilty feeling and enjoy him being here.

'Let me guess: thinking about Tia?' he asks, wrapping an arm round my shoulders.

'Sort of,' I say, leaning my head on his shoulder. It feels good.

'Once she's settled, you'll be messaging and chattering on Skype *all* the time. And, remember, she hasn't vanished – she's still there for you, just in a different way!'

I wonder if he's thinking for a second about Mum there: the missing part of our family who *did* vanish. I slip my arm round his waist and give it a squeeze.

'But, hey, Riley, there's something I was thinking when I saw you come up here,' he says, giving my shoulders a squeeze back. 'I know you and Tia have been coming up to the Angel all summer without an adult trailing along. But you're only eleven – it's not a great idea to be here by yourself, not now it's getting dark so early in the evenings.'

'But I'm twelve in a few days!' I point out, thinking of Friday, the day of my birthday, the day of the school trip to Wildwoods Theme Park. I unwind my arm from round his waist and hunch myself in.

'I know, honey, but you understand, don't you?' Dad says protectively.

My shoulders stiffen and I stare off tight-lipped at the view.

I mean, *yes*, I sort of get what he's saying. But doesn't he realize that he's just rubbed in the fact that I don't have a best friend any more? And not having a best friend (or *any* friend) means three things:

1) I don't have the freedom to go places on my own.
2) My birthday is going to be rubbish; I have no one to celebrate with at school.
3) The school trip will be even *worse*, cos I'll have to go on the rides solo. (How lame is that?)

'I'll just let Hazel know I'm with you,' says Dad, ending the hug he's giving me to fish his mobile out of his pocket.

Ha – like she'll care. 'OK, so she's not exactly a wicked stepmother,' Tia once pointed out, 'but she's not exactly *interested* in you, is she?' Too right.

In our 'family', I sometimes feel like I come below Alastair in importance, and, considering he's a lump of wood, that's pretty tragic.

No wonder I spend — I mean, spent *so much time round at Tia's*, I think to myself as I stare down at her empty house, the golden autumn leaves of the chestnut tree swaying in the gentle October breeze. Y'know, when I think of all the fun times I had there it breaks my —

Whoa!!

In a spine-tingling instant I'm jolted out of my moment of moping. Cos I'm staring at something that *can't* be right.

Silver-white . . . that's the colour of the blinding beams of light suddenly radiating from the windows of Tia's house.

'Dad . . .' I croak, feeling myself go rigid and cold against his warm, comforting side.

'Mmm, just a second,' Dad mutters, oblivious, his head bent over his phone.

Oh wow . . .

Every single window, from the living room to the kitchen and the loft bedroom where Tia slept till last night, *all* of them have an almost neon-bright gleam to them, as if an immense floodlight has been switched on inside.

'*Dad!*' I nudge him more urgently this time, forgetting I was cross with him a second ago.

'There, sent it. OK – what is it?'

But as soon as Dad lifts his head it's as if it – whatever *it* is – *knows* he's looking, and the light fades fast, as quickly as it had come.

'Tia's house,' I say, pointing with a trembling finger. 'The light in the windows was *incredible* just now!'

'Mmm, when the sun gets low, the reflections on glass can be really stunning,' Dad agrees casually, cos all *he's* seeing are the faintest twinkles and glimmers, as Tia's house reverts back to the empty, curtainless blank box that it's been since her family moved out this morning.

Oh.

So that's all it was? The sunset reflecting on the

windows for a few dazzling, glorious moments? Just a trick of the light . . .

But to me it seemed – dumb word, I know – sort of *magical*.

Feeling my juddering pulse slow to normal (and pushing the fear I felt to the back of my mind), I suddenly laugh at myself for coming up with something Dot might say.

Which reminds me. 'Hey, Dad – Dot thinks angels are moving in next door.'

'Really?' he says, getting to his feet and offering me a hand. 'I heard it was goblins!'

Hand in hand, grin matching grin, me and Dad head down the hill and home.

For a few moments I enjoy this tiny bubble of happiness, like I've just had a plaster stuck on my broken heart . . .

Hello, trouble

The school dining hall is mobbed.

I deliberately left it late to come here, since the busier it is the less likely anyone is to notice me.

At least, that was my plan.

'Hey – you dropped something!'

Usually people say stuff like that in a helpful voice, not one dripping with sarcasm.

But those people aren't Joelle Hunter.

'Um, thanks,' I say warily to Joelle, who passes me a folded piece of paper. It's an info sheet about Friday's school trip to Wildwoods.

The thing is, I have a sudden, sneaking suspicion

that it didn't fall out of my blazer pocket. There hasn't been enough time for the sheet to flutter to the floor, be scooped up and handed back, just like that. I'm pretty sure Joelle's done a perfect pickpocketing move on me.

But what would be the point in that?

'You must be absolutely *gutted* that Tia's left, Riley!' says Lauren, directing her comment my way.

For a microsecond I think her concern might be genuine – till I hear Nancy snort as she sucks the straw in her juice carton. And, great, now Joelle's joining in.

'Well, yes, I guess,' I answer as blankly as I can, nervously stuffing the folded paper back into my pocket with one hand, while balancing my food tray in the other.

I'm not hanging around to be sniggered at for whatever reasons these girls might have. But, just as I'm about to move on, Lauren talks again.

'*Loving* your eyeshadow, by the way,' she says, completely confusing me this time.

'Huh?'

'Red – it's a good colour on you.' Lauren smirks, then slaps a hand over her open mouth, pantomime style. 'Oh, I'm sorry, Riley! Are your eyes red because you've been *crying*? Over Tia leaving?'

You have to be deeply shallow to pass the time being casually cruel, don't you? And I'm not going to stand here for a second longer, being the butt of Lauren Mayhew's mean jokes.

So I leave.

Or at least I *try* to.

Suddenly I stumble on something, something that sends me lurching forward – and my lunch tray too.

I see it arcing upward, then swirling round in a perfect somersault.

SCHLOOP!

Goodbye, spaghetti Bolognese.

And hello, trouble . . .

'Hey, Riley!'

Uneven paving slabs, bumpy tarmac, tiny stones, windswept wrappers and general rubbish.

It's only now I hear the voice that I realize I've stared at the ground the whole way home from school. I must've crossed Meadow Lane with my head down, listening out for the beeps of the green man. As I turned the corner into Chestnut Crescent just now, it was as if my gaze was glued to the ground.

I look up and see Woody from Y7A.

'Uh, hi,' I mumble, checking for any signs of him snickering or snorting over yesterday morning's pavement splat.

'You all right?' he asks, sounding friendly. But, hey, so did Lauren this morning, till she put the boot in, so I don't trust him yet.

But in the meantime how exactly do I answer his casual question?

There's a bunch of stuff I could say, like I sat on my own all day, an empty seat beside me in every class. Or I could tell him that after yesterday's excitement with Mrs Sharma, everyone's gone back to blanking me.

In art I sat making calculations, figuring out how long it would take to save the airfare for New Zealand. (Answer: *too* long.)

Then in maths I sat doodling Tia's house, with Tia there in the loft window. (It didn't look right and I rubbed it out three times, ending up with a trio of ghostly faces instead of a smiley best friend's.)

'I'm all right,' I reply, shrugging all those other answers away, and wondering what he actually wants.

'Er, saw you at lunch.'

Oh, *that*.

Lauren had yelled at me for getting spaghetti Bolognese all over her new shoes – bypassing the fact that she'd deliberately stuck her foot out right in front of me.

'The way she was acting, I'd have gone and grabbed somebody else's lunch and tipped it over her *head*.' Woody smiles, booting a stone along the road.

I find myself smiling too, though I'm worried that I'm in *deep* trouble. There's no one to protect me if Lauren and her mates decide that it'd be fun to wind me up 24/7. There's no Tia to frighten them off, with one of her pretty but pretty fearsome scowls.

'So . . . heard from your mate, then?' Woody asks now, leaving the subject of my lunch-hall embarrassment alone.

I might have guessed *that's* why he's talking to me. Woody wants to hear all about Tia. I *knew* he had a thing for her . . .

That thought drifts away as my eyes settle on something unexpected.

Up ahead, all along our fence, is wave upon wiggly wave of glinting silver, as if someone has dipped their fingers in molten glitter and dragged them daydreamily along the wooden slats.

Someone like Dot, for instance.

And there she is now, playing in our garden with her little buddy Coco.

'Roll over!' Dot is saying, and pointing downwards at something out of sight.

'Is that your sister?' asks Woody.

'No,' I say.

It's too hard to explain that Dot is only my sort-of-stepsister. Dad and Hazel aren't married. She and Dot may have moved in *way* too quickly after Dad met her (at the hospital, where she stitched up the tip of his finger after he nearly guillotined it clean off cutting paper in his shop) but at least a wedding doesn't seem to be on the cards. Yet.

'ROLL OVER, Alastair!' Dot booms.

'He's not rolling over,' Coco is saying. 'Why don't you try a treat?'

'Hey . . .' Woody grins as he peers into our garden. 'Isn't that a –'

'Yes,' I say, hurrying through my gate and slamming it shut as if that'll block out his laughter.

I hope he's got the message and is leaving, but I'm not going to turn and check because my cheeks are on fire. I know what'll happen tomorrow morning. Those brain-dead Year 8 boys he calls mates? They'll all pass here, pointing and cracking up at me and my dumb kid 'sister' and her stupid lump of wood on a lead.

'Riley!!' Dot squeals now, passing the lead to Coco so she can come running over and give me a squeeze-of-death.

'Gently! I like my lungs the shape they are!' I tell her, trying to ease Dot's grip. Out of the corner of my eye I peek and see Woody ambling off up the street. Good. 'Dot, I said let go!'

I'm just about to try wrangling myself free again when I feel an odd sensation.

Tickle.

Prickles of tickles.

The hairs on my arms are standing up as if something or someone is stroking my skin with a feather-soft touch. It's just the chill of a sudden breeze, but it surprises me enough to spin back round in the direction of Woody, though I'm not looking at *him* any more. I'm staring at the silver estate car that's pulling up to the pavement.

It's parking.

Parking right outside number thirty-three.

Like a thunderbolt in my head, I remember a

conversation with Tia just last week. 'Hey, who's bought your house?' I'd asked as I'd helped her pack her beautiful room full of stuff into a huddle of dull cardboard boxes.

'Don't know.' She'd shrugged, not seeming to care. 'The estate agent just said it's a family.'

Well, that looks like a family car. I can't see anyone clearly, but there's more than one person inside. Enough to be a whole family?

'Hee, hee, hee!' Dot giggles, squeezing me tighter. I hardly notice; I'm not really concentrating on my squashed ribs at the moment. Cos the driver's door is opening.

And, oh . . . now there's a rumble as a removal van veers round the bend in the road and grumbles to a stop behind the car.

'Hey, looks like that might be the Angelos!'

Hazel's voice makes me jump as she appears in the doorway, the laundry basket in her arms.

'The Angelos?' I say, with Dot still wrapped round me like an affectionate apron.

'Mr and Mrs Angelo – the postman told me he'd already started delivering mail for them,' explains Hazel. 'I'd better get this lot in the machine. Keep an eye out and tell me what our new neighbours are like!'

It still feels odd to me when Hazel says stuff like that: 'our' neighbours, 'our' house. It's mine and Dad's. She and Dot just happen to share it with us.

Which reminds me, Hazel and Dad haven't seen the glitter trail on the fence yet. I might have to help Dot scrub that off before they do . . .

'Dotty! Dotty!' yelps Coco, cottoning on to what Hazel's just said. 'The angels are here! Look, look!'

'Lemme see!' shrieks Dot, dropping her hug-of-death and craning for a better look.

How funny, Dot and Coco are going to be mighty disappointed when an ordinary family pour out of the car. They're hoping for heavenly wings and harp backing music, and all they'll probably get is a harassed mum and dad with a squad of squawking babies and toddlers.

Yep, just as I thought, there's a perfectly normal-looking woman coming out of the driver's side now, and a matching normal man coming out of the passenger side.

They're wandering off to talk to three big, muscly blokes in canary-yellow polo shirts who've jumped out of the lorry cab and started thunking open its back doors.

Creak!

At that small metallic sound I focus again on the parked silver car, and see its back passenger door swing open.

A girl.

Tall, with waist-length wavy gold-red hair. She unfurls herself on to the pavement, brushing an unruly wisp off her face and blinking dreamily at the house – as if she's just woken up.

A short denim dungaree dress, that's what she's wearing, a thick, hand-knitted, pillar-box-red cardie slouched on top. Her longs legs like liquorice in black woolly tights and loosely tied ankle boots.

I guess she must be about twelve, same as me and Tia. (Well, just *me*, I suppose I should say now.)

'Is SHE an angel, Riley?' Dot asks me loudly, her nose crinkling, her arm pointing.

'Shhh!' I say sharply, shoving Dot's arm down. 'No, she's just a girl.'

'Well, what about HER?' Dot roars now, pointing her other arm in the direction of the car.

Another girl, following the first one out on to the pavement.

Shorter this time, wearing thick-rimmed black glasses, a long, baggy grey jumper, leggings and pumps. But what I *really* notice is the two tight dark buns on her head. They look a little like diddy Mickey Mouse ears.

What *she* seems to notice is her new home. Her eyes are narrowed, sternly scanning number thirty-three as if she's sussing the house out and seeing if it meets with her approval.

'No, Dot,' I whisper, pushing that arm down too. 'She's not an angel either.'

I reckon this second girl is about my age too . . . Twins, maybe? Non-identical, *that's* for sure.

'Then *this* one, Riley? What about her?' Coco joins in with the questions and pointing.

Huh? Someone *else* is clambering out of the rear passenger door.

It's a third girl. *Another* sister?

Skinny as a whippet, stubby white-blonde plaits, beaming a smile as she blinks. I feel myself blinking too. Her outfit's a bedazzling mix of a bright pink duffel jacket, denim shorts, stripy tights and sequinned baseball boots.

'Sorry, but she's just another ordinary girl,' I tell Coco, though her style is anything *but* ordinary. No one *I* know has the courage to wear colours that bright, shoes that sparkly – at least not all together. At our school all the girls mostly like to dress in shades of black and grey, in school *and* out.

This third new neighbour . . . although she's

quite dainty now I look at her, I'm sure she's around the same age as the first two girls.

Triplets?!

Is there such a thing as *extremely* non-identical triplets?

'They're WEIRD!' Dot suddenly announces loudly, while Coco gawps open-mouthed, her little button eyes desperately searching for signs of white feathers.

'Dot, they are *not* weird,' I whisper, desperate for my sort-of-stepsis to shut up.

Looking after Dot can be a bit like trying to herd snakes. It is *seriously* dangerous. She's the kid on the bus who'll shout, 'WHY'S that man got such a BIG NOSE?' or be the only person brave/stupid enough to hug a growling Staffie when other people cross the road to avoid it.

Still, I kind of know what Dot is getting at. Labelling these girls 'weird' is her five-year-old shorthand for 'different'. And, somehow, they *are* different. Different-looking from each other (the tall dreamy one, the stern-looking one, the pretty, ditzy one) but together they don't look like *anyone* in my neighbourhood. It's as if a small flock of flamingos has just elegantly flapped its way into a drab old penguin colony.

'They do TOO look weird!' Dot practically hollers.

OK, that's too much – I wrap a hand over Dot's mouth, and hope it looks like I'm giving her a sisterly hug if any of the girls look over. Not that they do. They're all drifting towards their house, staring, staring. The tall one gazes up at what used to be Tia's room, her hair flaming behind her in the breeze. The stern one steps slowly and surely up the path as if she's on a tightrope or a catwalk. The third girl goes to join the others, by way of the shrubs, gently running her fingers over the autumn foliage.

'Are they maybe people off the telly, Riley?' Coco suggests, spotting their specialness and trying to find her own way to describe it.

'I don't know,' I say with a shrug.

Perhaps they are. I could *sort* of see them as

actresses, or even models. If they were a few years older, I might have guessed they were in some cool, quirky girl band or something.

'Urgh!' I suddenly groan as Dot frees herself by licking the hand that I've slapped over her mouth.

'Look, Riley!' she trills, pointing frantically. 'The weird people HAVE GOT A *DOG*!'

I've been so busy failing to shush Dot that I hadn't spotted it hopping out of the car last.

But now I see it, and I'm going to get a closer look than I'd really like to, cos I'll have to go after Dot. She's just flown out of our garden, desperate to introduce herself and Alastair – being dragged behind by his lead – to the newest four-legged resident on the street.

Put it this way: since Dot won't bother to stop and wonder whether or not the new dog on the block might chew her or Alastair to pieces, *I* have to do her thinking for her.

'Dot! DOT!' I call out as I career round the gate and along the pavement, Coco trailing after me.

Too late – Dot's already thrown her arms round the dog's furry neck. But luckily it isn't a wolverine or anything too obviously carnivorous.

It's just . . . well, it's just a big blob of snow-blond downy fluff, like one of those poodle mash-ups. A poodle crossed with a golden retriever, crossed with . . . with a cloud? Whatever it is, it seems to be *grinning*.

'Dot!' another voice repeats, and I gaze over at the pretty, ditzy-looking girl, who is speaking. 'Dot!'

Is she taking the mickey out of me? I wonder to myself.

It's the sort of thing Lauren, Joelle and Nancy would do, and then smirk behind their hands and pretend they hadn't said a word.

But the girl isn't smirking; she's smiling as if she's just spotted a cute bunny or been offered a free ice cream with sprinkles. I notice that her Arctic-blonde plaits are fastened with cherry-shaped bobbles. (What would Lauren, Joelle and Nancy – our class's reigning queens of style as well as mean – have to say about those? Nothing nice, I'd bet.)

'Dot!' she says again in delight.

I think I'm staring too much.

But then so is someone else.

The girl with the black glasses and twin top-knots is studying me intently, as if I'm something extremely old and odd in a museum. I've never exactly known what the heebie-jeebies are, but now I feel like I've got a serious case of them.

'Uh, yes, this is . . . *Dot*,' I reply, nodding down at my sort-of-stepsister. 'And I'm Riley. We live next door.'

'Riley!' the blonde girl repeats in that same strangely delighted way.

She really is *taking the mickey out of me, isn't she?* I fret silently, feeling a tug of dread in my stomach. It's bad enough to have triple trouble in the shape of Lauren and her buddies at school – I could really do without having the same sort of hassle so close to home.

'What are YOUR names?' Dot asks bluntly, while pushing the fur off the dog's face so she can see its eyes. Eyes bright and shiny as two fivepences. The dog doesn't seem to mind and keeps right on grinning.

At Dot's question, the pretty, ditzy girl looks a little confused and glances sideways at the redhead.

Ah, wait a minute.

Are they foreign?

Maybe they don't understand English!

'Hello, Dot! Hello, Riley!' the redhead suddenly replies in what sounds like perfect, not-foreign-at-all English. 'I'm Sunshine, and this is Pearl.'

The one doing the talking, her voice is sort of . . . calm and chilled out. She sounds a bit like a much younger version of the spacey woman who used to do a kids' after-school yoga club at my primary.

But Sunshine? Her name is *Sunshine*? Really? *Sunshine* and *Pearl*?!

The girl who is Pearl gives a funny little bow and grins. (Coco might be on to something when she mentioned the telly – I could imagine this Pearl girl bouncing around on CBBC, no problem.)

'Hi!' says Dot, remembering her manners, even if I've temporarily forgotten mine.

'And *I'm* Kitt,' says the serious-looking girl in glasses.

If Sunshine is like the yoga woman, and Pearl is like some bubbly TV presenter, then who does this Kitt remind me of? Maybe Mr Thomlinson, our deputy head. He does a mean stare through his glasses when he catches you doing something you shouldn't be doing, like running down the stairs. Though he has never worn his hair in Mickey Mouse ear buns. Mainly because he's got hardly any hair at *all*.

But, hey, at least this third girl's name sounds more normal.

'Dot is short for Dorothea,' my sort-of-stepsister blurts out as she pulls a rainbow-striped clip out of her hair and uses it to pin back the fur from the dog's face. 'Is Kitt short for something?'

'Yes,' says the stern, staring girl. 'It's short for Kitten.'

Kitten?

Wow – I had no idea that could even be a name. And, if it is, this very assured, non-smiling person in front of me is *so* not a soft and sweet baby cat. Her parents – still currently busy with the removal van – got that *well* wrong.

'Ooh, Kitten! THAT'S pretty!' Dot chatters on happily, now studying a tag on the startled-looking fluffball's collar. 'I *like* your dog. Ha! "BEE"! That's nice too! Look, Coco, it's called Bee!'

'Hee hee!' giggles Coco, helping to strangle the dog with more hugs.

'Why did you call your dog BEE?' Dot demands, staring up at the girls.

'We just love bees,' Pearl answers for all of them as she starts to sway from side to side on her sparkly tiptoes, like she can hear music that we can't. 'It's the way they flutter about, with their beautiful wings!'

Pearl wafts her arms up and down a bit.

Coco gawps open-mouthed.

Dot frowns.

I can tell one or other of them is about to give Pearl a short lecture about the difference between buzzy bees and flutterbies.

They have no idea that she's teasing them, but *I* know that's what's going on.

Kitt turns to me and says sharply, 'She's joking.' But in a flat sort of voice that sounds anything but funny.

Why do I get the sudden feeling that she doesn't like me, when she doesn't even *know* me?

Then Sunshine speaks again, in her calm and chilled-out way. 'I like *your* dog,' she tells Dot, pointing down at Alastair.

Wait a sec – behind all that dreaminess, is she actually being sarcastic? I mean, I wouldn't blame her. *Most* people snicker at Dot and her driftwood dog, just like Woody did. But Dot simply beams proudly and wiggles her finger, indicating that Sunshine should come closer.

As the tall girl bends down, I notice that she has

the most amazing colour eyes, like the purply-greeny-blue of oil in puddles. I glance quickly at the other two – Kitt's are pretty startling too, the same shade as today's cloudless sky. Pearl's got her head down just now, but I think hers are pale grey, like a husky's.

'He's not real, you know!' I hear Dot whisper loudly as she points down at her precious wood-lump.

'Really?' says Sunshine, pretending to be surprised.

Please let her be kind to Dot and not burst my sort-of-stepsister's 'let's pretend' bubble. Let her act like Dad or Hazel when Dot tells them that there's a fairy living in her sock drawer or *me* when she announces I'm the person she'll marry when she grows up . . .

'Dot! Coco! Riley! I've got some snacks for you!' Hazel's voice drifts from the open kitchen window at the side of my house.

With a sense of relief, I yell, 'Coming!' and begin to shoo Dot and Coco towards the front steps.

'Riley Roberts!' one or other of the girls calls after me.

'Uh-huh?' I mumble, glancing over my shoulder, pretty sure it was Sunshine's voice I heard.

But the tall girl is standing still as a statue, except for her gently waving gold-red flag of hair. Beside her, Kitt's intense glare seems to be boring straight into my head. As for Pearl, her grin might be genuine, or she might be laughing right at me.

'What?' I ask again warily.

The three girls glance at each other with expressions I can't read and eyes that now seem almost *silvery* in this light.

'We didn't say anything,' Kitt announces, her metallic eyes mocking me from behind her glasses.

I clumsily back away, feeling my face flush pink. Prickles of embarrassment and confusion make the hairs on my arms stand to attention and sort of . . . vibrate.

As I hurry into the house, a jumble of disconnected thoughts tumble into my head all at once.

I'm not sure if I'm going to like these new neighbours.

I didn't imagine it: Sunshine *did* speak, I'm sure.

And exactly *how* could they have known my last name . . .?

Do I look like a dog?

'RAAAAAARGHHHHHHH!'

I wish the roaring was coming from somewhere in the house that was far enough away for me to turn over in bed and ignore it.

'*RAAAAAARGHHHHHHH!*'

Sadly, it's not. The wild animal seems to be on the other side of my bedroom door.

Reluctantly, I flip open my eyes and see two things . . .

1) an alarm clock with hands pointing to seven, and
2) Mum smiling at my curtains.

Mum's photo — I know this is going to sound mad, but last night I took it out of my knicker drawer and propped it up against the clock, so I could talk to her about stuff. About Tia, about how awful and lonely school is, about how rubbish my birthday and the school trip to Wildwoods will be, and about the girls who've moved in next door.

It helped. Sort of.

I mean it made sense of the last name thing, at least. Cos some time in the dark it dawned on me that Tia's parents probably left a bunch of useful info for the estate agent to pass on to the new owners of number thirty-three. Useful info like the names of the neighbours, which is how those girls would've known I'm not just Riley, but Riley *Roberts*.

And so eventually I must've nodded off without realizing, even though there was plenty of stuff I *hadn't* figured out. Stuff like whether the Angelos were really winding me up, or was I freaking out for no reason? Maybe I was. I haven't slept much lately, always tossing and turning, dreading Tia leaving.

I blink myself more awake and, with Mum's smile so close, for a second I feel OK. Well, as OK as you can feel first thing on a Wednesday morning, with roaring going on nearby.

'RAAAAAARGHHHHHHH!' roars a tiger, barging into my room with a clatter and dragging my bedding off me.

'Go away, Dot,' I mumble, scrabbling for the squishy comfort of my duvet but finding it gone, tumbled somewhere at the end of my bed.

'RAAAAAARGHHHHHHH!' the tiger roars again, her paws/arms flailing wildly. If I had the energy, I'd grab the sleeves of her stripy all-in-one PJs and tie them in a knot.

'You've had a bit of a lie-in, haven't you, Riley?' Dad calls brightly from the doorway. 'But it's time to rise and shine, sleepy head!'

Huh? How could I be sleeping? I have no bed covers and am being attacked by a ferocious five-year-old.

'Morning,' says Hazel, breezing into my room like she owns it and scooping the terrible tiger into her arms. 'Right, time for big cats to get dressed. And big girls to get some daylight in their rooms!'

With one arm curled round Dot, Hazel uses her free hand to yank my curtains apart and let the early-morning light flood in. Ouch.

'Have you seen the time, Riley?' Hazel says in her usual brusque and efficient way. 'You're going to have to get a move on if you don't want to be late for sch– Oh!'

She seems to be a little surprised by something she can see through the window.

'What's up?' asks Dad, re-appearing in the doorway.

'Hurray!' squeals Dot, and starts hammering her tiger paws on the glass.

All right, so I'm exhausted but I'm curious, and

get out of bed to see what's happening in the outside world.

'Wow, *they're* keen!' says Dad, who's beaten me to it, laughing.

Flip goes my tummy when I see who everyone's looking at. Sunshine, Kitt and Pearl.

They're standing by our garden fence, dressed (sort of) in the uniform of my school. With their dog at their feet. And all four of them – if you count Bee the dog – are staring up here.

Wait a second . . . are they *waiting* for me?

It's only 07:03 according to my clock. Oh no . . . I read it wrong! It actually says 08:03, which gives me next to no time to have breakfast, get washed and dressed, and panic about the new people waiting to walk me to school.

Help!

But the next half an hour goes by in a blur of school-morning mayhem. Before I know it I'm creaking our gate open, adjusting the pink ballet hairband I borrowed from Dot to hide my bald spot, and saying a shy 'hi' to the three girls who've been hovering here, even though Hazel went out to ask them if they were OK ('Yes, thank you'), or if they wanted to come in ('No, thank you').

'Hello, Riley,' says Sunshine brightly.

'We've been waiting for you,' Pearl states, though that's pretty obvious.

Kitt does nothing but stare. Hard.

I'm trying not to stare back but, wary as I'm feeling, I'm kind of intrigued by her and her sisters' version of the Hillcrest Academy uniform. I mean, our school is pretty relaxed; it's not as if you get suspended for wearing the wrong shade of grey skirt or having your nails painted clear with a faint hint of pink, like at some stricter schools.

But what are people going to make of Sunshine's flurry of multicoloured butterfly clips holding her tumbling waves off one side of her face?

Or Kitt's mad-but-fun Mickey Mouse buns?

Or Pearl's stripy tights and sequinned baseball boots?

The thing is, *I* might not know quite what to make of my new neighbours yet, but I do think they *look* pretty interesting . . . in a kooky, cute way. And I'm suddenly so glad that finally *someone* in my year at school won't be looking either boring (like me) or dressed as a wannabe clone of Lauren, Joelle and Nancy, with their flicky long hair and short, short skirts (like almost every girl in Year 7).

Speaking of Lauren, Joelle and Nancy, I bet they'll give Sunshine, Kitt and Pearl the once-over, then rip them to shreds behind their backs. Though I have a funny feeling that the Angelos aren't going to care too much about that . . .

'Bye!' A voice drifts over, which belongs to Mrs Angelo. I recognize her from yesterday, when she got out of the car with her husband. 'Have a great first day!'

The three mismatched sisters wave at the very ordinary woman in the doorway of number thirty-three and then turn expectantly to me.

'Shall we go?' Sunshine smiles my way.

Right. So it seems they've volunteered me to be their guide for the morning, whether I'm up for the job or not.

'Uh, OK,' I mumble timidly.

The girls fall into step beside me, saying nothing.

All that nothing is unnerving. My normal short walk to school with Tia always passed in a babble of chat in two seconds flat. Today, if this carries on, it'll feel like two *hours*.

The further we walk, the longer the silence; it makes me stress about what's going through their minds. Despite Sunshine's smiles, maybe they didn't want to walk with me to school in the first place. (Well, Kitt didn't look exactly keen.) Thinking about it, maybe Mrs Angelo *told* them to.

Should *I* say something? But *what*? I fret as we turn out of Chestnut Crescent and approach the traffic lights on Meadow Lane, the zoom of traffic in our ears.

Mrs Angelo — I could mention something about *her*, couldn't I?

'Your mum seems nice.'

There. I did my bit. Now it's *their* turn to talk.

But instead Pearl laughs, though I'm not sure if it's at what I've just said or cos the red man's just turned to green at the crossing.

'That is *so* funny!' she giggles, copying the arms-out pose of the green-man outline on the traffic lights.

'No, it's not,' Kitt snaps at her sister. 'And anyway she's not our mother.'

OK, that second snap was aimed at me.

I concentrate on crossing the road, turning my hot face away, since I don't understand what Kitt's just said, or why she had to say it that way.

(A worry wriggles into my brain: she really doesn't like me, does she?)

As we reach the safety of the opposite pavement, it's Sunshine who speaks next. 'Frank and Sarah Angelo are our foster carers,' she explains.

'Oh . . .' I say in a small voice, stumbling slightly with surprise as we go to turn into the small road that leads to the school gates.

Well, *that* makes sense. It could be why Kitt's so spiky, couldn't it? *And* why the 'sisters' look nothing alike.

Except for those shades-of-blue eyes, of course . . .

But, before I get a chance to absorb that latest chunk of confusion, I suddenly notice we have company. *Furry* company.

'Er, did you know Bee was following us?' I say, hesitating and pointing to the dog at our heels.

Bee continues padding along, grinning up at me, tongue lolling.

'Oh, it's fine – he'll go when he's ready,' Sunshine says easily.

Huh?

How can Sunshine trust her pet to find its way back to a brand-new house, across a busy junction too? Pets aren't that independent. Not unless they're witches' familiars or something.

And, let's face it, this doggy fluffball doesn't look much like the sort of animal companion your average witch would go for. And serene Sunshine doesn't look too much like a witch. I don't think . . .

'So are all the other people at school as nice as you, Riley?' Pearl asks out of the blue as if everything is one hundred per cent normal.

I'm feeling wall-to-wall flustered, cos absolutely *none* of this seems normal to me. And I'm not sure if Pearl's spoofing me or not.

'They're all OK, I suppose,' I answer vaguely, staring down at a content-looking Bee. 'Apart from a few . . .'

'Like who?' asks Sunshine.

I lift my head and see she's gazing intently at me. Oh no, I am *so* not going there.

I mean, I don't really know these girls, and already they're twisting my head in knots. With *my* luck, I'd have a full-on moan-a-thon about Lauren and co., and next thing Sunshine, Kitt and Pearl would be joining forces with them, *doubling* their mean power.

So I'm just going to shrug off my comment and say it was nothing, to be on the safe si–

'STOP!' barks Kitt. '*Stay* there!'

I look round to see where Bee is and what he's doing – then realize Kitt is actually talking to me. Me! I mean, do I *look* like a dog?

'It's all right,' I say, spotting that her sisters are staring at the quiet road, with only parked cars in it. 'It's safe to cross he– *Whoa!!*'

As I automatically go to step off the kerb, Kitt lurches forward and grabs my arm tight – *really* tight.

'What are you doing?' I ask, shocked.

'The car,' Sunshine says as I flip my head round and see a navy-blue people carrier suddenly drive off fast, really fast, without signalling. The woman in the front is busy waving at the boy she's just dropped off and not looking at the road. Right this second, if Kitt hadn't yanked me back, I'd have easily been within thudding distance of the car bonnet.

But how did Kitt guess that the stupid driver was about to move?

Trembling, I'm just about to ask when Kitt says something else: 'Bye.'

And – still catching my breath – I watch Sunshine, Kitt and Pearl drift off towards the school gates, without another word.

I might be standing in a sleepy suburban dead-end on a bright autumn morning, but I'm shivering as if I'm in the middle of a Siberian storm.

And no one seems to care, apart from the fuzzy dog that's now nuzzling my shaking left hand . . .

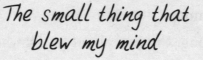

The small thing that blew my mind

I don't know how long I've been standing here on the pavement.

Probably no more than a few seconds.

Long enough for the comforting snuffling nose to disappear, that's for sure.

I shake myself out of my shock when I hear the bleep-bleep of the pedestrian crossing back on Meadow Lane. Hurrying to the corner of the road, I'm just in time to see Bee happily pad on to the opposite pavement, tail wagging, watched by confused passers-by and head-scratching drivers.

Then I'm jolted by the distant sound of the bell

and run, run, run towards school, through the gate, across the crowded playground, and land breathlessly in the crush of the hall.

There they are: up ahead, on the stairs. Sunshine's rippling river of red-gold hair, Kitt's funny little buns, Pearl's stubby snow-white braids.

I shuffle and slide between bodies and schoolbags, desperate to catch them up, even if I don't know what to say when I do.

How about: 'You saved me, Kitt.'

Or: 'How could you have known what was going to happen?'

Maybe even: 'Why did you act like it was no big deal and then walk off?'

Those are all questions I really want answers to, but I'm too shy – or maybe *scared* – to come out and ask. Instead, as I finally wriggle my way up and fall into step beside the girls, I mumble, 'Um, thanks, Kitt.'

'For what?' she snaps at me, taking me by surprise.

Those two blunt words feel like a slap in the face,

and I immediately speed up, suddenly very keen to get away from these confusing sisters, or foster sisters, or whatever they are.

But as I try to go I feel a gentle touch near my wrist and turn to see Pearl grinning as much as Kitt was scowling just now.

Though it's Pearl who's got my attention, it's Sunshine who speaks. 'Can you take us to our class, Riley?' she asks. 'It's called "y7c".'

'Uh, yeah,' I say hesitantly. 'That's actually *my* class.'

I don't know why I'm so surprised; there may be five form classes in Year 7 but mine is the only one with space. Last term, Ben Adams got expelled for setting fire to Amy Chung's pencil case with a Bunsen burner in science and Amy Chung's parents moved her to a different school cos they didn't want her to go to a place that had someone like Ben Adams as a student (even though he'd got expelled). And of course as from this week there's also the Tia-shaped hole in y7c.

'So where do we go?' asks Sunshine as I peel away at the first floor and begin to lead them along a glass-walled corridor.

'The library,' I tell her, noticing for the first time the effect the Angelos are having on everyone who's passing. Boys, girls, from our year to much older – their eyes are glued on these three odd but oddly exotic creatures. No one is sniggering or gossiping; they're just looking, looking, looking.

Pearl smiles and wiggles her fingers at them in a wave. Sunshine drifts along, not even noticing the attention she and her sisters are attracting. Kitt, however, notices something altogether different.

As I raise my arm to push open the library door, I see her frowning at the sleeve of my blazer. She looks . . . well, *furious*.

'Oh,' I say, spotting five small silvery fingerprints near the cuff. 'That'll be Dot. She gets glitter *everywhere*.'

For some reason my explanation doesn't seem to have impressed Kitt. Her gun-metal grey eyes are still glowering through her black-rimmed glasses. (Didn't I think they were more *blue* before?)

Flustered, I push my way into the already busy library, self-consciously brushing the glitter from my navy blazer, since it seems to bother Kitt so much.

'We're usually in our form class now,' I start to explain, 'but cos our teacher – Mrs Sharma – is off, we've been told to come *here* for registration.'

The rest of Y7C had been a blurry swarm of chattering students when we came in, but I'm sensing their voices fading away, their eyes fixing on me and the girls I've walked in with.

It's like what happened out in the corridor just now. And it's silly, I know, but I feel a shiver of excitement, like I'm hanging out with pop stars or something.

'Wow!' says Pearl, almost skipping along a set of shelves and dragging her fingers across the top of a long line of Jacqueline Wilson books.

Sneaking a peek out of the corner of my eyes, I

see some of my classmates follow Pearl's every move, her every skip, taking in the matching twinkles of her smile and her baseball boots.

'I like the pictures,' says Sunshine, gazing at jumbled rows of Year 7 artwork plastered around the library walls: the self-portrait project we did when we first started at Hillcrest.

Sunshine has no clue that the casual flick of her ribbons of red hair was just studied this second by virtually *all* of the almost silent students of Y7C.

'*You*,' says Kitt, walking up to and pointing at the blow-up black-and-white photo I took of myself.

My cheeks flush pink, realizing that everyone in the library may now suddenly be scrutinizing it, since Kitt is.

As for the photo itself, I look blank and bland in it, I reckon. But that's probably because it's got Tia's amazingly colourful chalk drawing to one side of it, tropical flowers and hummingbirds filling up every part of the paper that isn't her pretty face. On the *other* side is Lauren's self-portrait, hair long and yellow with streaks of gold paint swooped through, looking like she's some Greek goddess or something.

Pearl joins us, her eyes scanning Lauren's picture. 'Is that the girl over there?' she asks, pointing her thumb over her shoulder, but not looking back herself. 'The one with the upside-down mouth?'

I don't know if Pearl's got eyes in the back of her head, but I turn to see Lauren saunter into the library, flanked by Joelle and Nancy.

With a toss of her long blonde hair, Lauren hesitates, sensing something's going on.

It's not hard to see why; the library is a teacher-free zone at the moment, and yet no boys are roaring, no girls are yakking.

Lauren's over-mascaraed eyes automatically follow everyone's gaze. And Pearl is right: her expression is so sulky her mouth makes a shape the complete *opposite* of a smile.

All of a sudden Lauren's sights lock on us, and then, *blam*, she regains her composure and sashays our way. 'So, Riley, who are *they*?' she asks, nodding her head at Sunshine, Kitt and Pearl.

Behind her, Joelle – her naturally curly dark hair ironed flat – stares dully on, while Nancy ogles my neighbours from under her long fringe and nibbles at her black-painted nails.

'Who are *you*?' Kitt asks straight back, before I've had a chance to answer.

Uh-oh.

Joelle snorts, Nancy gasps, but more importantly Lauren bristles, her narrowing eyes indicating that a nasty remark is about a nanosecond away.

But someone else gets in there first.

'Welcome to my world!' shouts Mrs Mahoney, the learning resources manager, stretching her arms wide as she stomps out of her office.

By next week, we'll have a new form teacher assigned to us in Mrs Sharma's absence, but in the meantime Mrs Mahoney is loving the excitement of having a captive class all to herself.

That's *bound* to change once the boys start being

cheeky and the girls start chatting. Which they might do, if they all manage to stop staring at the three people by my side.

'Anywhere you like! Park yourself down!' Mrs Mahoney calls out, pointing to seats and tables.

There's a scuffle of feet and a screech of chairs on lino. Me, Sunshine, Kitt and Pearl slide round a table at the back of the room (good) but find ourselves parked just behind Lauren and her friends (bad).

I try not to catch their eyes, but I know Lauren and Joelle and Nancy are looking our way as they take their seats. You can feel their individual radars homing in, picking up every detail, studying every angle of me and the new girls.

'Right, we have a few things to talk about today, including Friday's school trip to Wildwoods Theme Park, of course,' Mrs Mahoney announces, to cheers and hurrays. 'And then there's the holiday homework project Mrs Sharma set you, which I'm sure *everyone* has brought in with them!'

'Uhhh . . .' I sigh out loud, and a lot more loudly than I meant to.

We were supposed to have written or made a presentation about the most memorable day we'd had during our first half-term at Hillcrest. But I'd been too wrapped up in moping over Tia to remember about it.

'Oh dear,' mutters Lauren, turning round to look at me with mock sympathy. 'Forget to do your homework, did you? Tsk, tsk . . . *You'll* be in trouble, Riley Roberts!'

Great. I've forgotten to do my assignment and now Lauren's *loving* making me feel bad about it.

'Oh, Riley *has* done it,' Sunshine suddenly says, a serene smile on her face.

I fix her with a quick what-are-you-on-about panicked look, but Sunshine blithely carries on.

'It's just not quite finished yet, is it, Riley?'

I don't know if Sunshine is coming to my rescue because she *likes* me, or is winding Lauren up because she doesn't like *her*.

'Uh, not qui–'

'Shush!' Mrs Mahoney's voice cuts across my words and the rustle of homework projects being dragged out of schoolbags. 'But, before all that, let's start with some new students who are joining your class today. Girls – you know who you are. Can you come here, please?'

Appearing completely unfazed, my new neighbours get up. They go and stand in front of the long library check-out desk, which is laden with books, plus some sad and faded yellow roses in a vase. By the mournful look of the flowers, they must've been there since before the holiday.

'OK, everyone,' says Mrs Mahoney, 'can we put our hands together and give a big Hillcrest welcome to Sunshine, Kitt and Pearl!'

The main noise is the enthusiastic blast of applause.

Secondary to that is the hubbub of curiosity.

The third is one bold, easily heard word.

'*Freaks.*'

No prizes for guessing who said that.

But something pretty unexpected has just happened: no one laughed.

Instead, the whole class turn and frown at Lauren, like she's just kicked a puppy. I spot Lauren bristle, stunned for once not to be the Queen of Everything.

Meanwhile, Sunshine, Kitt and Pearl act like they either didn't hear or don't care about Lauren's remarks. Sunshine's head is tilted to one side, the fabric wings of her hairclips fluttering prettily. Kitt's face is still and unreadable. Pearl appears to be humming to herself while her fingertips brush over the dead heads of the roses in the vase.

'Well!' booms Mrs Mahoney, trying to gloss over any unpleasantness. 'I'm sure *everyone* will help you settle in, girls! And now . . .'

As Mrs Mahoney drones on, I rummage in my bag for my school notebook, thinking I might sit here at the back unseen and quickly scribble some ideas down for the project I haven't remotely started, no matter what Sunshine just said to Lauren.

'Riley,' someone hisses at me.

I pretend not to hear, and concentrate instead on flipping to a blank page in my notebook. 'Riley!' the hiss comes again, more insistently.

I know it's coming from Lauren, but I simply tug at my pink ballet hairband and blank her.

'*Riley!!*'

Sigh . . . OK, so I can't ignore her any more. I glance up and see Lauren hanging over the back of her chair, her waterfall of blonde hair draped over her arm.

What? I mouth.

Pound, pound, pound goes my heart, but I remind myself that she can't hear that.

In answer to my 'what?' Lauren throws a thumb over her shoulder, towards Mrs Mahoney, just as I tune into what she's saying. 'So how about it? Let's have a round of applause for Riley Roberts!'

Thunk!

The shock of being singled out by Mrs Mahoney makes me drop my notebook on the floor. I reach down to grab it and –

Clunk!

– slam my forehead on the table in front of me.

'Come on, Riley!' Mrs Mahoney orders me cheerfully, waving me upright.

I struggle to stand, swaying with waves of shyness and shock (and maybe concussion), and see my whole class, their faces swivelled in my direction.

What *is* this all about?

Out of the corner of my eye, I can't help noticing three particular girls giggling their pretty heads off at my expense . . . and I'm *not* talking about Sunshine, Kitt and Pearl.

'Lauren – you too,' booms Mrs Mahoney, jovially waving her to her feet. 'You can do the interview over on the sofa in the corner while the rest of us get on.'

Huh? *What* are we doing? I should've been

listening and not scribbling, I fret as my thunked head thuds.

But all I can do is follow Lauren as she sashays her way over to the slightly frayed and stained red sofa that Mrs Mahoney has mysteriously exiled us to.

'Ready?' Lauren smirks at me as she settles herself down and sticks her phone and a digital voice recorder down on the small space between us.

'For what?' I ask, knowing that she's totally buzzing on me being so clueless.

'For your interview, of course!' she says with a roll of her eyes. 'About what happened with Mrs Sharma?'

Lauren's talking to me like I'm a particularly stupid toddler. But I don't understand why she's talking to me at *all*.

'I'm on a try-out for the *News Matters* team,' she explains wearily. 'You're my trial interview. So you'd *better* be good.'

I don't want to be 'good'. I don't want to be

interviewed by anyone, especially Lauren. And I don't want to be in the online school newsletter for everyone to ogle at.

'So go on, then,' says Lauren, clicking a button on the recorder and flopping back on the sofa. 'What's it like to be "a hero"?'

She holds her fingers in the air to mimic quote marks. For some reason that small gesture really throws me; it's as if she's suggesting I've made up the whole Mrs Sharma drama. Or that I'm not a 'real' hero, which I know I'm not anyway.

Whatever she means exactly, I'm now in a total muddle and feel even *less* able to speak. 'I didn't . . . I mean . . . it wasn't like a big thing. I guess.'

'You don't think Mrs Sharma nearly *dying* is a big thing, Riley?!' Lauren says in fake surprise.

'She nearly *died*?' I ask, absolutely stunned. Had something happened to her at the hospital that I didn't know about?

'Well, no, but she *could've*. Her *or* her baby!' Lauren says with a shrug of her shoulders. 'I mean, there could've been complications, or *germs*. It can't exactly be hygienic to deliver a baby in a cupboard.'

'But she didn't *have* her baby in a cupboard!' I reply. 'We were in Mr Bradley's office . . .'

'So you're saying you actually *delivered* Mrs Sharma's baby? Cos *I* heard you weren't even *there*. That it was a medic who helped her give birth, not *you*.'

'Well, no . . . I mean, yes!' I protested.

This conversation was making my head go twisty. It was like the one I had a couple of days ago with Dot, except instead of having it with someone small who loved me, I was having it with someone my size who didn't even *like* me.

'Well, what *did* you do?' Lauren demands, sounding slightly exasperated.

My scrambled brain replays the scene in the site manager's room at high speed. The stuck doorknob. The panic. The hair-pulling. It was all a blur, like it took place over just a few moments, not ten *loooonnnngggg* minutes.

How could I put all that into words? Why isn't Tia with me? She could explain it all calmly and coolly, looking Lauren straight in her heavily mascaraed eyes, daring her to trip me up with tricky questions.

But there's no Tia; there's only little useless me, sitting here with a thumping heart and matching forehead.

'I spoke to her about panting,' I say finally.

It's suddenly like the moment in the gym on Monday morning – a long second's silence before giggles erupt, though this time it's just Lauren and not the entire class, at least.

CLICK!

The fingers of one hand cover Lauren's laughing mouth, while the index finger of the other flips the recorder button to off.

'That's *it*?' I say.

'Uh-huh.' Lauren nods, the sarky smile fading, being replaced by a look that seems to dare me to challenge her.

What's Lauren on about? It doesn't feel like she even asked me any *proper* questions. But maybe I should just be glad it's over with, since it was as much fun as being trapped in a lift with a wasp.

I begin to move, to go back and join the rest of the class, when Lauren speaks again.

'Cheese!' She giggles, and – *FLASH!* – I'm instantly blinded.

'Thanks for the photo, Riley!' says Lauren, in a voice that sounds as if she's smirking, though I can't see for the white whorls in my eyes.

Listening to the tippetty-tap of Lauren's black pumps as she walks away, I try to blink my sight back, my heart thundering at the unfairness, her meanness, my uselessness.

Oh, I wish, I wish, I wish . . .

I wish Tia hadn't disappeared to the other side of the stupid world.

I wish I could stand up for myself.

I wish I wasn't alone.

I wish –

'*It's going to be all right, Riley.*' I hear that comforting, far-away whisper in my ear as the white mist clears and my vision begins to return.

And the first things I see clearly are the faces of Sunshine, Kitt and Pearl, staring earnestly at me with their eyes the colour of skies on different days. Mrs Mahoney is showing them some info sheets about using the library, but, since they're staring my way, I don't think they're listening.

As I blink some more I see something else. A small thing that blows my mind.

Pearl: her fingers are still idly playing with those wilted yellow roses.

But under her tender touch something seems to have happened to them. A few minutes ago, they were floppy and dead. Now their sunny heads are stretched up towards the fluorescent lights on the library ceiling.

Hey, I'm the girl who's good at imagining things that aren't real, right?

But this is different.

This is *happening*.

And it's not just Pearl coaxing a bunch of supermarket flowers back to life.

What about Sunshine casually brushing off the fact that her dog has some completely impossible in-built homing device?

Or Kitt's power to see into the future, since she *knew* to stop me before the car moved outside school earlier?

Their eyes too . . . It's like they're different colours every time I look at them.

Just *who* have Mr and Mrs Angelo ended up fostering? The daughters of illusionists, like those people on TV magic shows who can levitate on the street or make viewers watching at home believe they're stuck to their sofas?

Suddenly, I have a brand-new wish.

I wish these girls hadn't moved in next door, because they're *seriously* freaking me out . . .

Come inside . . .?

Approaching our house, I drag my fingers along the fence, tracing the wavy lines of glitter.

At least where yesterday's wavy lines of glitter *were* . . . Had Dad or Hazel wiped them off? Or maybe it rained in the night and washed them away. But, hey, there's plenty more where *that* came from, I think, remembering the sparkly silver fingerprints on the cuff of my blazer this morning, and the marks on the front door on Monday morning.

Dot was going to *have* to have a glitter amnesty, or I'd be raiding her craft box and confiscating it myself . . .

Bang! Bang! Bang!

I hesitate with my hand on the gate.

The hammering is coming from Tia's house. OK, the Angelos' house.

I step back, just enough that I can see down the side of the building to where the old chestnut tree stands huge and gnarled in the garden.

Oh! I've been spotted spying. Not by Mr Angelo, who's bent over a stack of wood, but by Sunshine, Kitt and Pearl, who all wave while Bee barks. (So he obviously *did* find his way home from school this morning . . .)

I manage a wiggle of my fingers and hurry inside, overcome by shyness and uncertainty *again*.

After the weirdness going on in the library this morning, I stayed well away from my new next-door neighbours, and they seemed not one tiny bit bothered by that.

At break and lunch I'd seen them drifting, watching, looking, whispering.

In class I'd slouched down in my seat, while

everyone else – including Lauren, Joelle and Nancy – sat upright and open-mouthed as Y7c's three newest students breezed through every question in every subject, as if maths, physics, French or whatever were as simple as nursery rhymes.

And I'd deliberately taken my time leaving after the home bell blasted, so I wouldn't run into them. (I stood and read an announcement on the noticeboard saying Mrs Sharma and her baby girl were doing fine. Five times.)

At last I'd scuttled out to find no Sunshine, no Kitt, no Pearl – no *Bee* – waiting for me by the gates, which was a relief. Or disappointing. I couldn't figure out which . . .

'Hey, Alastair,' I say now to the lump of wood in the doggy bed as I push open the front door.

Pleased to see me, Alastair rolls over on his back to get his tummy tickled (*not*).

'Hello?' I call out more loudly, hanging my schoolbag from the peg in the hall.

No answer – the radio is up loud in the kitchen and Dot is up louder still.

Padding silently along, I stop just before the kitchen doorway and peek inside, like a spy in my own home.

The slight, twanging pain in my chest – maybe it's the first sign of heart problems, but I think it's probably a twinge of jealousy cos Dot is perched on the kitchen counter, singing her heart out and wafting a washing-up-liquid bottle around. It's got wonky-shaped wings taped to the sides and black and red paint splodges decorating it.

Hazel is smiling at her dippy daughter while trying to undo some sticky tape that's tangled in Dot's hair.

That cute mum-and-little-kid scene, it never happened for *my* mother and me. How sad is that?

And the way Hazel is gazing at Dot, as if she's the most amazing, adorable person in the whole wide world . . . how great would it be to have someone look at *me* that way?

OK, so Dad does it from time to time. At least he did it a lot more before he got together with Hazel. Now his smiles and love have to be shared around the three of us, and sometimes it feels like I get the smallest piece of the 'family' pie.

'RILLLEEYYYYYYY!' roars Dot, suddenly spotting me. 'Look, I made a rocket at school today. *SWOOOOSHHH!!*'

'Great,' I say as I wander closer to take a look at her handiwork. 'But fancy keeping it away from me? You've made enough mess on my jacket already!'

I'm talking about the glitter on my cuff, but Dot is oblivious and doesn't bother to react. She's *way* too busy swooshing her rocket around.

'Stay still, Dottie, darling,' says Hazel, trying to sound strict but half laughing. Then as an afterthought she adds, 'How was school today, Riley?'

Hazel always asks the questions she thinks she's supposed to ask, without being remotely concerned about my answers. When Dad first introduced us I guess he hoped we'd be all best buddies and sharing girly chats together once she and Dot moved in, but it's somehow never happened. Like I say, I'm polite to Hazel, and she's polite back.

And so it's only polite for me to answer her question.

But how?

Do I tell her the truth?

That I spent the day getting told off by teachers for daydreaming/not paying attention in class because I was either . . .

a) fretting over who I could contact on the *News Matters* team to ask them not to run Lauren's non-story about me

b) writing lists of ways I could get out of going on the Wildwoods Theme Park school trip on Friday

c) wondering what on earth Tia would make of the Angelos . . .

I hadn't ended up with an answer to my first two noodlings, but I figured I did know what practical, no-messing Tia would say about the last one.

'Are you serious, Riley? There's nothing "witchy" about Sunshine and her dog! She must've just trained him really well.'

'Honestly, you NEVER notice anything. But I bet Kitt is just super-observant, so she heard the car engine rev in the street and guessed it was about to move.'

'The roses? I bet you a tenner Mrs Mahoney had put fresh water in the vase five minutes before you all turned up in the library – THAT's why they all perked up. It was nothing to do with Pearl!'

See? That's why Tia was like my guardian angel – she could protect me from my sometimes mad self by telling me what was really happening, and what I should think . . .

'Riley?'

Hazel is staring at me, waiting for an answer.

So how was school today? Well, because I don't want Hazel to think I'm mucking around/having a brain meltdown, *this* is the answer I give her: 'It was OK.'

'That's nice,' she says, turning back to the sticky, wriggling mess that is my sort-of-stepsister. 'Dottie, stay still, darling!'

Since I'm not really needed, I mooch through to the living room, and plink on the computer.

The screen radiates into life. And with a tap or two I'm checking, and there are precisely . . . let's see . . . *zero* messages for me. (Sigh . . .)

It's no surprise, not with all the flights and travelling and stopovers Tia and her family have to do over the next few days, but I still flop my head on to my arms on the desk and let out such an enormously long sigh that I might just deflate altogether.

And then –

Tickle.

Prickles of tickles.

The hairs on my arms are standing up, the same as the other day, when the Angelos were moving in.

I lift my head a little and look left and right,

listening, hardly breathing. There's no one, there's nothing.

Slowly, I straighten up. And just as I come face to face with the computer screen, out of nowhere a single tiny white feather flutters down and lands on the keyboard.

BING-BONG!!!

The doorbell goes, making me jump.

'*I'LL* GET IT!' I hear Dot yell as she thunders down the hall.

I pick up the feather and swirl it round between my fingers, wondering where on *earth* it's come from.

'RILEY, IT'S FOR YOOOOOOOOU!' Dot positively screams, probably deafening whoever's at the door.

As I walk into the hall, at first I only notice that Dot's also got a decorated cereal-packet jet-pack strapped to her back with string. Then I see someone bent down just inside the doorway, gently stroking Alastair in his doggy bed.

'Hello, Sunshine! Come on in!' says Hazel,

appearing behind me and rubbing her hands dry on a tea towel.

What makes Hazel think Sunshine would *want* to come in?

What makes her think *I* want Sunshine to come in?

And what will I *do* with Sunshine if she does? Come in, I mean.

'Riley?' Hazel is frowning at me.

'Uh, hi,' I say hesitantly, shoving the feather into my skirt pocket.

'Hi!' smiles Sunshine, standing up again and staring straight at me.

Eek! I don't really know what I'm supposed to do or say.

'Why don't you show Sunshine your room?' Hazel suggests on my behalf, ushering her inside.

'Um, yeah, sure,' I mumble feebly. 'It's –'

'– THIS WAY! HURRY!!' squeals Dot, grabbing Alastair by the lead and clunking him step by step up the stairs behind her.

'That is *my* room!' Dot yelps, pointing a finger at her polka-dot and bunny-poster-filled bedroom. 'And *this* is Riley's!'

Our tiny tour guide stands in the doorway with arms outstretched and bits of space paraphernalia gently detaching from the jet-pack.

Sunshine glances around, and begins to mooch and meander, gently touching books and nail varnishes, gazing up at the dangling beads of the plastic chandelier that hangs from the ceiling.

But, while I'm not much of a host, Dot is loving every second of showing off my stuff.

'It's pretty, isn't it?' she says, flipping the light switch on.

'Wow!' Sunshine gasps softly as the different-coloured plastic segments of the chandelier glow.

She's being sarcastic, right?

But then her purply-greeny-blue eyes are wide and innocent. Those eyes, her floating, fluttering gold-red hair . . . she might just be the most beautiful girl I've ever seen.

'And see THESE?' blurts Dot, waving her arms towards my pinboard of pictures as if she was presenting them.

'Dot, we haven't finished cleaning you up,' says Hazel, appearing at my bedroom door. 'You've got paint all over yourself.'

'But —'

'But nothing. Come on . . . leave the big girls alone.'

Nervous now, I nibble a strand of my mousy hair to a backdrop of 'not fair's and thunks (Alastair making his way downstairs).

Sunshine's back is to me as she slowly examines each photo.

I'm about to ask her why she stepped in and lied to Lauren about me doing my project earlier — but she gets in with a question of her own first.

'What is this place?' she asks, and I shuffle self-consciously to her side to see what she's talking about.

Ah, it's the photo I took of Tia cartwheeling by the Angel.

'That's up at Folly Hill,' I explain, pointing out of the window.

Sunshine tilts her head to one side in confusion, pale red waves falling away from her face like the softest of velvet.

Oh. She doesn't get what I mean!

Hasn't her family noticed that they've bought a house beside a huge mound of earth?

'Here,' I say, motioning her over to the window.

Now she can see it: the looming green of the hill rising behind the roofs, the glint of the white-marble Angel on her plinth on the summit.

'Tia and me used to lie on our backs up there and watch the clouds,' I say softly, scared that my voice might crack as I mention my best friend.

And then *whoosh* . . . out of nowhere a sudden, startling idea whizzes into my head. It must be the combination of the pinboard and the view, cos now I've thought of my overdue holiday homework, and what it can be about.

It's that day in September, when everything changed.

I took photos, didn't I?

Of Tia lying back with her eyes closed.

Of the Angel watching over us.

Of Tia sitting up, telling me the awful news about New Zealand.

Of her face, trying to smile, to make it OK.

Of her breaking down when she saw me start to cry.

Of the two of us hugging, the Angel behind us, the camera on timer propped up – capturing the end of an era.

Yes, *that's* what I'll submit for my school project. It had to be the most important day in my first half-term at school – even if it *was* for all the wrong reasons.

I feel a flurry and flutter of excitement – I'll let the photos tell the story, with no text. I'll print them out when Sunshine leaves, mount them on a big bit of card, and think of a great title. Actually, maybe

I'll ask Dad to copy them at his shop, on bigger paper, like he did for my self-portrait –

'We'd like to go up there,' Sunshine interrupts my thoughts, speaking – bizarrely – in plural. 'We like being up high. That's why we're all in the loft room.'

'What ... you, Kitt *and* Pearl?' I check, so surprised I forget my nervousness, forget about my project.

The thing is, Tia's house has four bedrooms, enough for each girl to have her own room.

'Mmm,' Sunshine murmurs dreamily. 'And that's why Frank, our foster dad, is building us *that*.'

Now she's pointing across at the broad branches of the chestnut tree in her garden – where Mr Angelo, in jeans and fleece zip-up top, is balanced precariously, planks of wood under his arm and a hammer in his hand. Watching him intently from below are Kitt, Pearl and Bee.

'You're getting a *treehouse*?' I check again.

The chunky chestnut is perfect for it, and I'm

amazed no one – including Tia's family – has ever built one there before. But it's a funny thing to do when you've only just moved into a new home, isn't it? I thought Mr and Mrs Angelo might still be busy unpacking boxes, not doing a sudden stint of outdoor DIY. Especially since Mr Angelo doesn't look too steady. In fact, he's pretty wobbly.

He's stepped one foot down on to a branch that doesn't look strong enough to take his weight.

He's realized his mistake at the last minute and pulled his foot back where it was, but too fast.

I see a flash of red trainer as his foot starts slipping off the mossy old bark of the main branch and, uh-oh, now his hand launches out to the side, trying to grab on to the tree trunk.

But in the panic of the moment his hand doesn't find it.

Now he's dropped the hammer from his other hand and . . . and it looks – oh, help – it looks like he might – oh, please no! – *fall*!!

Just as a choked squeak of alarm lodges in my

128

throat, the girls' foster dad miraculously manages to grab hold of the branch above and steadies himself. He looks puzzled, staring at the empty hand that was holding the hammer a moment ago.

Stunned, I turn round to see Sunshine's reaction. And it's the strangest thing.

She seems to be silently, madly mouthing something. Words? A desperate prayer maybe?

But her face doesn't look desperate; her expression is completely calm, just as it always seems to be.

And, hey, she's not looking at her foster dad, she's staring down at her sisters in the garden.

Kitt is mouthing something back, while Pearl does a little twirl of pleasure, hammer in hand!

Then – *snap* – the mood of the moment is gone; Sunshine turns and smiles sweetly at me as if nothing just happened. Down on the grass a stony-faced Kitt takes the hammer from Pearl's hand and matter-of-factly reaches up to pass it back to Mr Angelo.

'Well, better go help out with the treehouse!' Sunshine says brightly, turning to go.

Huh?

Did I just see what I think I saw?!

Of course I *want* to ask Sunshine about her foster dad's near-accident, but I'm scared it's going to be like yesterday when I thought I heard her say my name, or when Kitt pulled me back from the car. She might shake her head at me, denying it all, and I'll feel even *more* like I'm going a tiny bit loopy.

So, completely tongue-tied, I nearly let Sunshine leave without another word. *Nearly.*

As I pad down the stairs behind her, something stirs inside my befuddled brain and I find I *am* able to ask her one question at least, even if it has nothing to do with Mr Angelo.

'Er, Sunshine . . . why did you come over in the first place? Did you want something?'

I hadn't thought to ask earlier, and neither had Hazel; she'd simply ushered her inside.

130

'Oh, I just wanted to see your photos!' Sunshine says with a bright beam over her shoulder. 'Bye!'

'Right . . . bye,' I reply as she heads out of the door and down the path.

It's only as I close the door that *another* obvious question pops into my head. How did she know about the photos . . .?

Sort ofs and shocks

'Can we? Can we? Can we *please*, Riley? *Pretty* please! Can we?'

When Dot asks if we can take Alastair out for a walk I usually say no.

Not because I'm mean, but because people tend to stare when you're dragging around a stick on a lead.

But today, just this once, I don't mind. Sunshine went home a few minutes ago, leaving me with a head full of tangles, and I'm desperate to get some fresh air.

'Where are you two going?' Hazel asks as she watches me and Dot put our coats on.

'Where are we *THREE* going, you mean,' Dot corrects her mum, nodding at the lump of wood on the end of the lead she's holding.

'*Three*, then!' Hazel smiles indulgently.

'Up to the Angel,' I tell her. If the brisk October wind up on Folly Hill can't blow away head tangles, I don't know what will.

'All right – but don't be long,' she replies, looking at the kitchen clock.

'We'll be back in half an hour, before it starts to get dark,' I promise, thinking of Dad's recent chat with me.

I help wrestle Dot's padded jacket on over her jet-pack and we set off, trudging up the flinty path that meanders towards the Angel and –

Oh.

Look who's beaten us to it.

Sunshine must have taken her sisters (and dog) up here almost as soon as she got back from ours.

'*Don't you get it, Riley?!*' Tia would've said. '*Sunshine guessed you were into photography, cos she saw that self-portrait you took – the one in the library!'*

Well, OK, maybe that made sense, but Mr Angelo nearly falling, his foster kids' super-strange reactions . . .

'BEEEEEEEEEEEEEEEEEE!' shrieks Dot, running as fast as she can towards the snow-blond fluffball on legs.

Bee happily bounds over to meet her, and even courteously attempts to sniff what might be Alastair's bottom.

The two dogs and Dot are joined by Sunshine and Kitt, while Pearl . . . Pearl is twirling on the spot, arms wide, face to what warmth there is in the watery October sun.

'Oooh!' She laughs as her twirling brings her straight across to me. 'Hello!'

Everything about Pearl seems to twinkle – her laugh, her eyes, the sequins on her baseball boots.

'Hello,' I answer warily, wondering if she's just too pretty and sweet to be true. I mean, people meeting someone like *Lauren* for the first time would think she was a gorgeous, smart girl, not a twisted, mean-mouthed bully. You can never trust first impressions, can you?

'It's nice up here!' Pearl says with a happy sigh. 'We *really* like it.'

I start to soften. Anyone who likes this special spot of mine can't be all bad, can they?

'But what's *that* supposed to be?'

Pearl's eyes are on me, but one of her hands is pointing slightly behind her, to the right. The only thing over there – apart from an amazing view – is the Angel.

'It's . . . uh, an angel,' I say simply.

Pearl frowns, then makes an unexpected sound. 'Prrrrrrrrfffffff!'

Now it's *my* turn to frown. She just *sniggered*?

'What did you think the statue was?' I ask, bewildered.

I mean, big wings: *tick*.

Hands clasped together: *tick*.

Dress like a floppy sheet: *tick*.

Eyes to the skies: *tick*.

What *else* would she be?

You know, I bet the long-ago lord of Hillcrest House had her made so she'd watch over his land and protect it or something. Don't think he'd have expected a twelve-year-old girl to get the giggles over her one day in the far-off future.

'It's just that I've never seen –' Pearl goes from grinning and chatty to silent all of a sudden, as if she's been caught doing something she shouldn't.

She's now glancing in the direction of Dot, the dogs and her sisters. Kitt is staring our way. Hard.

'Never seen what?' I tentatively ask, wondering what it is about me that makes Kitt dislike me so much.

'No, nothing. I forget,' Pearl says unconvincingly. Then a small smile breaks out on her face again. 'She's funny.'

'The Angel?' I ask, confused. Again.

'No – your sister.'

'Dot? Yeah, she's great,' I answer as I watch her tearing around with Alastair thunking behind on his lead. 'But she's not my sister. She's my *sort-of-*stepsister. It's complicated.'

I hope I can leave it at that. I'm not really up for the whole Dad/Hazel/my-mum-died story, not with people I hardly know.

'Like us,' Pearl replies, and begins her twirling again.

As she spirals away from me, I guess she's as reluctant as I am to get into messed-up family stuff.

I have no idea what sort of tangle of chaos and social workers it took for Pearl and the two other girls to end up here, and I'm not about to ask. Not yet.

But right now I find myself wishing I had my old rubbish camera with me. I'd *love* to snap Pearl spinning, spinning against the background of the green grass and cloud-spattered sky, with the marble-pale angel in the background. It would make a great photo.

'Uh-oh.' That's Pearl, suddenly twirling to a halt, and staring straight at Kitt.

Kitt, in turn, is staring at the brow of the hill.

But why? There's no one and nothing there . . .

Ah, except *here* comes someone now.

It's as if Kitt sensed them coming, I think to myself as I absently watch Bee bound off, Dot lolloping after him, dragging Alastair by his lead.

The someone is an old lady, who gazes off happily at the view – at the *exact* time my little sort-of-stepsister crosses in front of her, the stupid stick dog hidden by the longish grass.

'Oof!' cries the old lady, tripping over Dot's non-dog and landing in an unladylike pile of crumpled coat, groaning.

'I'm sorry, I'm sorry, I'm sorry!' Dot starts to cry, realizing what she's done.

We 'big' girls are all there at once, Pearl hugging Dot, Sunshine and Kitt on either side of the woman, taking an elbow each, my chilly bare hands holding her two woolly-gloved hands.

'Oh my!' she mutters, letting herself be hauled upright.

Seeing that the old lady is steady enough, we all gently let go.

'Are you all right?' I say.

'Yes, thank you, dear. No damage done!' she jokes, patting her puffy-as-candyfloss hair. 'Just a bit of a dent to my pride. Oh! Your face!'

The candyfloss lady has lost her smile and is frowning at me now. She's spotted the bruise above my eyebrow, from thumping my head on the desk earlier. Or maybe my hairband's slipped and she's seen the bald spot. Or maybe she's seen both . . .

'You know, dear, you look *exactly* like someone I used to know,' she says, a smile of recognition suddenly blooming.

I do?

'I used to buy flowers from her, years ago.'

Oh.

'Now what was her name? Emma? Amy? No, no. *Annie* – that's it! Annie's Posies, that was what the shop was called. Do you know the place I mean? Used to be right by the station. Do you know her?'

'No,' I reply, shaking my head more than it needs to be shaken. 'Um, glad you're OK. But I'd better get going.'

Grabbing a puzzled Dot by the hand, I hurry away from the Angel, from my neighbours, but most especially from the old lady, her candyfloss hair, and her heart-stopping questions about my mother . . .

Unless . . . what if?

'Look, think of it like some great tragic love story,' says Tia as she paints my toenails the same shade of fuchsia as her bedroom walls. 'Two people who are crazy about each other, then fate steps in and cruelly steals one of them away . . .'

'Yeah, but it's not a story,' I say with a sigh. 'It's my life.'

'Well, technically, it's your mum and dad's,' Tia replies. 'You were only a baby when your mum had her accident. You have no memory of it. Your dad saw it happen, so no *wonder* he's still broken-hearted and never wants to talk about her.'

Yes, I think, flopping back on to Tia's bed. *It's just that I feel like I'm not allowed to know my own mother, or even to love her . . .*

'Riley!'

I shake myself out of my daydream. My daydream of hanging out with Tia in her loft room, talking about life, love and long-gone mums. I missed Tia so much last night. After what that old lady said to me up on Folly Hill I was *desperate* to talk it over with someone. But there was no one.

'Riley!'

I blink, and find myself staring at . . . *me*!

'Riley! Are you *so* speechless at seeing yourself on screen?' asks Mr Forbes, our English teacher.

The latest *News Matters* is being projected on the whiteboard.

My so-called interview and photo, courtesy of Lauren, is up there for everyone to see.

Or crack up at.

And no wonder.

The photo is terrible. There's the egg-sized lump

on my forehead, and my pound-coin-sized bald spot is in clear view. It's like a still from CCTV camera footage, the sort of thing that gets flashed up on one of those crime programmes on telly.

As for the (very) short paragraph underneath, it makes me sound like I have all the brains of a tin of soup.

SURPRISE SCHOOL BABY!

This week, Mrs Sharma shocked herself and everyone by having a baby in Mr Bradley's office, after student Riley Roberts locked them both in and couldn't open the door.

'I'm not a hero,' Riley told this newsletter. 'I just talked to Mrs Sharma about pants.'

Luckily Mr Bradley came to the rescue and phoned for an ambulance. Mrs Sharma and her baby are doing very well, in spite of everything.

As the class round me howls with laughter, I keep re-reading the words.

'*Riley Roberts locked them both in*' – no I didn't!

'*In spite of everything*' – meaning *me*?

And I'm not even going to go *near* the pants . . .

I turn round and look for Lauren. There she is, raking her fingers through her hair and giving me a 'whatever' shrug.

'All a bit of fun,' Mr Forbes mumbles un-convincingly as the end-of-lesson bell trills and he waves his hands to quieten us down. 'Can I remind you all that you need to go to the library now to get more details of tomorrow's school trip from Mr Thomlinson?'

With rumbles, scrapes and squeaks of chairs, we're all up and filing out.

Then I suddenly hear a cheeky wolf-whistle – coming from Joelle.

'Looking good in your photo, Riley!' Lauren says with a grin.

Nancy just sniggers over her bitten black fingernails.

There's such an almighty squish of people in the

corridor – with ALL the various Year 7 classes spilling out of classrooms and heading for the library – that I can't do what I really want, which is to peel off and go and hide in the loo. There's no point in me even *being* at the meeting, because I am NOT going on the trip. I'm going to fake being ill tomorrow and celebrate my birthday by moping in bed . . .

But, stuck shoulder to shoulder in the solid river of students, I let myself be reluctantly dragged along in the current – till I feel a stare boring into my head.

'Yes?' I mumble at Kitt.

What, is she going to *talk* to me now? Well, that's strange, considering she said exactly *nothing* all the way to school this morning, looked at the homework project I showed her sisters without a single word.

'That photo of you was bad.'

OK, so I *get* that Kitt doesn't like me. Maybe she's jealous of her sisters meeting someone new, or maybe there's something deeply unpleasant about me that I'm unaware of. Whatever the reason, I don't need the snidey remark. That's a Lauren tactic, and after what just happened in Mr Forbes's class I've had about as much of Lauren as I can take today.

Make that this week.

Actually, this *term*.

I stare down at the ground, hiding the fact that my eyes are stinging, that tears are looming. If she hasn't got anything nice to say, why doesn't she just leave me alone?

As if she can read my mind, Kitt slows down and slips backwards, swallowed by a tidal wave of blazers and ties.

Meanwhile I find myself unwillingly propelled into the library and quickly try to squash myself against the back wall, wishing myself invisible in case the other Year 7 classes have already seen the online newsletter and want to have a laugh at my expense too.

'Come on, everyone – take a seat or find a

space, please!' Mrs Mahoney shouts, with an accompanying clap of her hands. 'I want complete silence before Mr Thomlinson gives you your instructions for tomorrow!'

There's never usually complete silence this fast, but, as it's our properly strict deputy head who's going to be doing the talking, the quiet that descends is impressive.

Yet, just along from me, Sunshine, Kitt and Pearl are having a full-on whispered conversation. Only their whispers are so amazingly soundless that they might as well be *lip-reading* each other.

For a few minutes, while Mr Thomlinson drones on (and I don't listen), I try to fathom the Angelo girls' mute chat. From their body language it seems like Kitt's telling the others what to do, but what's new? She talks, they listen, nod, add a comment or two.

What *is* going on with those gi–

'Riley?'

No! It's happening *again*.

I've drifted off with my thoughts and not realized that a teacher, or a librarian in this case, is saying my name.

Please, please don't single me out! I plead silently with Mrs Mahoney. I don't want the whole of my year group to turn and stare at me . . .

'Riley Roberts?' Mrs Mahoney persists.

'Here she is!' someone booms in my ear, and I turn to see Woody from Y7A holding both his arms up, his hands pointing down at me. His goofy grin fades as he checks out my expression and realizes I'm neither grateful nor amused.

'Ah, there you are!' Mrs Mahoney beams, while rifling through a pile of something on her desk. 'I thought you'd disappeared on us, Riley!'

'I *wish* . . .' came a snidey remark (Lauren), followed by two matching sniggers (Joelle and Nancy).

'Shush, now!' Mr Thomlinson orders, before any other giggles can ripple around the library. 'Let's listen to what Mrs Mahoney has to say, shall we?'

'Thank you, Mr Thomlinson. Well, now that we've heard all about tomorrow's exciting trip, I just wanted to use this opportunity to thank everyone in Y7C – the form class I'm looking after – for getting their holiday projects in. I've had a quick look through, and there're lots of very *interesting* pieces of writing.'

Oh no! Did it *have* to be written? I didn't realize that! I've messed up; I'm going to get hauled up about it and laughed at *again*.

'But I wanted to say a word about *your* submission, Riley. The way you've chosen to present it, it's really very powerful.'

'Pffff!' comes a snort from one particular person.

But it's quickly lost in a shuffle of feet and a screech of furniture as the whole of my year leans forward to see better.

Help! I want to curl up and die . . .

They'll read the six words of the title and think I'm pathetic. I mean, *How Do I Be Only Me?* It sounds like I'm totally sorry for myself, doesn't it?

'Hmm ... yes, these are *very* good, Riley!' Mr Thomlinson agrees, peering through his glasses at the big board of black-and-white photos. 'And, as with your self-portrait on the wall, I really like that slight silvered effect you use.'

What? I don't use a silvered effect, *or* silvered photo paper ... But, looking over at my photo on the library wall, I see that it *does* seem to have a faint shimmer to it.

Is it to do with the way the sun's streaming in the library windows? Cos it's having an odd effect on quite a few of the pictures Blu-tacked up there. For instance, Tia's bright chalks have faded to something more pastel. And Lauren's face ... I don't know what kind of paint she used but it's as if it's *melted* or something, distorting her prettiness into something odd, like a twisted reflection of a fairground Hall of Mirrors.

Or am I doing my usual trick of imagining things that can't be true?

I shake my head a little and get ready to

look again, but I'm distracted by a loud burst of noise.

It's the sound of someone clapping.

And the sound is coming from the direction of Sunshine, Kitt and Pearl.

They're gazing over at me, one scowling, one smiling, one grinning, but they're *all* applauding me.

And now Woody's joined in, with a whoop on top, which gets *everyone* – with the exception of three people – to join in.

A room, a huge room of people rooting for me . . . it's the opposite of being invisible, and I'm not sure I like it, but then again I'm not sure I don't either.

It feels kind of good to be cheered on. Like there's a . . . tiny *glow* deep inside me. I glance around at all these interested, smiling faces, and suddenly feel, well, a little bit *stronger*.

'Quite right. Well done, Riley! Much deserved!' Mr Thomlinson booms, clapping along too, before holding his hands out for calm. 'And it's actually reminded me, I have a message for you from the headteacher.'

Bang goes my sudden confidence; my insides have just turned to half-set, watery jelly.

What have I done?

'He'd like you to take a bouquet of flowers to Mrs Sharma at the hospital at lunchtime, on behalf of all the staff and students,' Mr Thomlinson explains. 'And you can choose a friend to go with you.'

OK, now *there's* my problem.

I don't *have* a friend.

In a panic, I blink my way around at all the gawping Year 7s, knowing that all of them are aware of the fact that the one person I'd choose is a few thousand miles away.

Unless . . .

I mean, what if . . .?

Maybe I don't *have* to be just me.

I look over at Sunshine, Kitt and Pearl.

They've stopped clapping and have dropped their arms by their sides, their job done.

They're all staring directly at me, in a blaze of blue eyes.

'Mr Thomlinson?' I say hesitantly.

'Yes, Riley?'

'Can I take *three* friends, please . . .?'

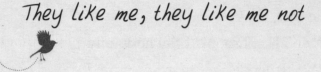

They like me, they like me not

'Ooh!'

It's as if the flowers are talking.

But of course it's Mrs Sharma, who's disappeared behind the vast bouquet I've just presented to her from the staff and pupils at Hillcrest.

It's an amazingly beautiful jumble of cream lilies and peach roses and all sorts of other stuff I don't know the names of. (My mum, Annie – the florist that she was – would have taught me them, I expect, if she was still around.)

'Who's a lucky girl, then?' says a nurse, noticing that Mrs Sharma has been eclipsed by a greenhouse-worth of petals. 'Here, let me take them from you and I'll try to find you a vase big enough!'

As the flowers and the nurse disappear, I get a proper look at Mrs Sharma, and blush. It just seems wrong to see a teacher in their pyjamas, like visiting your dentist and finding they're wearing their swimsuit.

'Thanks again, Riley, they're gorgeous,' she says. 'And what a lovely surprise to see *you* two here!'

Yes, there are two of us, not four like I'd dumbly hoped for back in the library . . .

'Yeah, well, I nearly wasn't – I'm the substitute!' says Woody, doing one of his funny but lame jokes that used to get Tia groaning, though I can't say I mind them too much.

'Well, I'm very glad to see you, Woody, however it's come about!' Mrs Sharma laughs as she leans over and scoops a baby bundle from the see-through plastic crib by her side. 'And exactly how *did* it come about?'

I hunch down deeper in the padded visitor's chair as Woody – perched happily on the end of the bed – launches into his explanation.

'So the head wanted Riley to visit you today, and she was told she could bring a friend,' he begins. 'Then she asks these three new girls in her class to come along; only they say *no*, so Mrs Mahoney suggested *me*, since I'm your favourite-ever geography student!'

Woody had told me that in the taxi on the way over here, the one the school office had organized for us. Mrs Sharma might be the form teacher for *our* class, but she was Mrs Sharma of the geography department to Y7A.

'Oh, so my daughter's not the *only* new girl in town?' Mrs Sharma interrupts with a joke of her own. 'Here – you can hold her, Riley, while you tell me about your new friends.'

'They're not my friends,' I tell Mrs Sharma, tentatively taking this three-day-old person in my arms.

I can't make any sense of the way Sunshine, Kitt and Pearl act with me, and I'm tired of trying. One minute they seem to be interested in me, on my side even. Wasn't that what the applauding was all about?

Next minute, I'm being told 'No thank you – we're not going to come with you' by Kitt, in front of everyone in the library.

Can you imagine how that felt?

'Why don't you tell me about them anyway?' Mrs Sharma says chattily to me.

'Uh . . . they're called Sunshine, Kitt and Pearl – they moved into Tia's house.'

'Interesting names!' says Mrs Sharma, raising her eyebrows ever so slightly. 'So are they triplets?'

'Foster sisters,' I say, and feel a pang of sympathy for the Angelo girls, and whatever sad stories brought them into care. But then I remember that very public *no thanks* and fizzle with hurt and humiliation again.

'So . . . might they *develop* into friends, do you

think?' Mrs Sharma asks, sounding hopeful on my behalf.

Well, Sunshine and Pearl maybe. In fact, today in the library, they seemed pretty disappointed when Kitt had barked out her *no thanks*. But as neither of them spoke up against her I guess that means what Kitt says goes.

'I don't think so, no,' I reply in a small, sad voice.

'Yeah, but they're all right, though,' Woody butts in. 'They don't seem to be phased by you-know-who, eh, Riley?'

'Who's that?' Mrs Sharma turns and asks me, sounding like the concerned form teacher she is, when she's not busy having babies, that is.

'It's just . . . well, Lauren Mayhew's been a bit, y'know,' I say, not sure where to start.

'Is *this* what you're talking about?'

Mrs Sharma lifts her mobile from the bedside cabinet, and holds it up for me to see. The screen is displaying the *News Matters* article.

'Mmm,' I mumble, wincing at the sight of my awful photo.

'Oof,' groans Woody, sliding up the bed to take a look. (Great.)

'Lauren hasn't quite got the details right, has she?' Mrs Sharma comments. 'And as for that photo . . . oh dear! It's not quite up to *your* standard, is it, Riley?'

For a second I think of Kitt and her snidey remark about the bad photo. Did I get defensive and cut her off too soon? Like Mrs Sharma, was she maybe about to make the point that my photos were really good in comparison to Lauren's? Hmm, probably not . . .

'You should've seen Riley's project today, Mrs Sharma,' Woody adds. 'She's done these brilliant prints of her and Tia up on Folly Hill, with the Angel and everything. They're awesome.'

'Really?' says Mrs Sharma, raising her eyebrows, at either Woody's over-the-top compliment or my over-the-top blushes. 'Well, why don't you offer your photography services to the school newsletter team, Riley?'

What Mrs Sharma is saying is very flattering, but:

a) I can't see Lauren being overly excited by me joining the *News Matters* team too, and
b) I'm not properly listening to her.

That's because there's a bloke with a ponytail hovering at the entrance to the room.

'Here we are!' says the nurse, breezing back over to Mrs Sharma's side. 'One beautiful bunch of flowers in water, plus *another* visitor!'

'Mrs Sharma – we spoke on the phone earlier,' says the ponytail guy, suddenly holding up a professional-looking camera. 'Would it be all right to take a photo of you and the baby now for our feature?'

Mrs Sharma nods. 'Oh yes! And you couldn't have timed it better. Riley, this is Jamie from the

Herald. And, Jamie, this is Riley, who came to my rescue when I went into labour.'

'Yeah?' says ponytail guy, who I had already figured was from the local newspaper, since I just caught sight of his identity card dangling from a lanyard round his neck.

'Perfect!' he says. 'Riley – could you stay exactly as you are, holding the baby? And, Mrs Sharma, if you could lean over in your bed a little towards Riley. And, Riley, lean your head towards Mrs Sharma . . .'

This position he's putting us in, it's going to come across *so* stiff and corny. If *I* was taking the photo, I'd ask questions, get us talking, so we'd seem relaxed and happy in the shot. Not like two human Leaning Towers of Pisa.

Uh-oh – Woody is snickering, so I'm now *sure* this pose looks as stupid and awkward as it feels.

'Any chance of a smile, Riley?' ponytail guy quips.

But my mouth isn't cooperating. Help . . . this is

going to be as bad as the photo in the school newsletter! It's just going to be a chance for even *more* people to see some silly schoolgirl who didn't do anything special or heroic.

Even the baby knows I'm a fraud; she's starting to wriggle and grizzle.

Oh to be able to close my eyes and dream up my mum's voice telling me it'll be all right.

Instead I've got to stare down the lens of a camera while fighting the urge to get up and run away.

And then . . .

And then I feel prickles of tickles as a cool hand softly strokes, strokes, strokes my arm, and I start relaxing in spite of myself.

I turn to give Mrs Sharma a quick thank-you glance for her comforting touch, and see that her hand . . . well, it's nowhere near me. In fact, *both* her hands are clasped together in her lap.

Snap!

'That was lovely, Riley, with you looking up at

your teacher,' the photographer says encouragingly. 'Very natural!'

Ha.

Just like lots of things happening this week, it's more like *super*natural . . .

Floating, flying, free

I'm good at imagining things.

And sometimes that upsets me.

But the comforting touch I imagined at the hospital earlier, it made me happy.

I haven't had much experience of that sort of thing, but it felt like a mother's touch. So it's no surprise that I haven't been able to get Mum out of my mind since then . . .

'What are you looking for?' asks Hazel as I scrabble about in the cabinet in the living room.

'I think there's an old frame in here,' I mutter as I move around piles of ancient DVDs, unidentified cables and only-come-out-at-Christmas posh placemats.

'Uh-huh? And what are you going to put in it?'

The frame I'm thinking of has been in here since before Hazel came to stay, same as all the stuff in here. I don't think it's really any of her business, but since she asked . . . 'My mum's photo,' I tell her.

My head might be inside a cabinet, but I can picture the disapproving look on her face. Especially since she's gone silent.

'Got it,' I say, grabbing the pretty white wooden frame that's only slightly bashed at one corner and closing the cabinet door against the now teetering contents inside.

'I'm just not sure how your dad will feel ab—'

TAP! Scrabble, scrabble, SCREECH!

I hate being rude and I really don't want to discuss this with Hazel so I'm relieved to hear the strange sort of clattering, scratching noise at the door.

'Probably Dot,' I say, hurrying into the hall.

I'm expecting to see my sort-of-stepsister or her little friend Coco trying to do something random, like post snails or possibly *Alastair* through the letterbox.

What I *don't* expect when I open the door is a smiling dog.

'Bee?' I say in surprise.

'Woof!'

The snow-white fluffball turns round and heads down the path – then, realizing I'm not following, he looks over his doggy shoulder, fixes his ice eyes on me and woofs again.

'Um, I'm just . . . just going out for a minute . . .' I call back to Hazel, leaving the frame on the floor propped against the wall and pulling the door closed behind me.

Feeling slightly mad, I follow the padding Bee down our path, on to the pavement and round into the garden at number thirty-three.

'RILEEYYYYYY!' Dot's voice yelps at me. 'WE'RE HERE!!'

My first instinct is to look up at Tia's old bedroom window in the loft, where we'd sit and daydream and chat for hours upon lazy, happy hours. But there's no one at the open window, just a waft of a white muslin curtain flapping gently in the breeze.

'OVER *HERE*!!' Dot yelps again.

Tilting my head to the right, I see that Dot, Coco, Sunshine and Pearl are in the amazing treehouse built by Mr Angelo, which is nestled in the sprawling branches of the giant chestnut.

There's no sign of Kitt. Phew.

'We sent Bee for you,' Sunshine says, her chin resting in her hands, her gold-red hair tumbling over the wooden rail. 'Fancy coming up?'

After what happened in the library this morning my first instinct is to say no thanks, same as Kitt said to me.

But, with no stern-faced Kitt in sight, I realize I *do* want to climb up there.

Still, what I'd love even *more* than that right now is to go up to the loft – my spiritual home.

'Or we *could* show you our room, if you want?' Pearl giggles down at me.

'Um, yeah,' I mumble, reeling from the coincidence. But then coincidences happen all the time. Especially round here . . .

With a step, step and jump, Sunshine and Pearl have padded down the ladder – one pair of undone lace-up boots, one pair of sparkly baseball boots – and landed silently on the grass beside me.

Scuttling in their wake are Dot and Coco.

'Are you two coming?' I ask, pointing to Tia's house.

'They can stay; Bee will look after them,' says Sunshine.

'He won't let anything happen to them,' Pearl chips in. 'He's a guardian dog.'

'*Guard* dog,' Sunshine quickly corrects her sister. 'Coming, Riley?'

'Don't worry; we're FINE, Riley!' Dot assures me as I hesitantly begin to follow Sunshine towards the house. 'I'm the mummy, Coco's the daddy and Bee's going to be our baby!'

With a gentle hand on my back from Sunshine, I find myself stepping through the cheery cherry-red doorway into a house I barely recognize. The sienna walls of the hall are now white. The African art Tia's parents had plastered all the way up the stairs is replaced with, well, *nothing*. The red stair carpet has been torn up and the steps are now sanded and varnished pale wood.

As we turn on the first landing and take those last twenty steps up to the loft, my heart is pounding. Judging by what I've already glimpsed, it's going to look very different. It's bound to seem smaller too, with three beds packed in instead of one.

'Ready?' asks Sunshine, outside the oh-so-familiar door.

'Ready,' I reply, taking a deep breath and preparing to be saddened.

I don't quite see Sunshine's hand push the door open and yet it's swinging wide and revealing . . . a *wonderland* of white and dreamy blue.

'The walls!' I say, marvelling at how they're the

exact shade of the sky outside the window. And there's something about that colour that makes the room feel enormous, much bigger than when Tia was here – about three times as big – even *with* the extra beds fitted in.

The floor has been sanded and bleached the colour of driftwood. The white metal bedsteads are covered in duvets and pillows as puffy and enticing as clouds.

All this, and the flapping muslin curtains I already spotted from the garden . . . it makes me feel almost dizzy, as though I'm flying, floating, free.

'Is it strange to see it so different?' Sunshine asks gently.

I can't help but laugh at that.

'No, I – I love it!'

Sunshine and Pearl exchange pleased smiles as I glance around at the blank but calming walls. Except they're not *completely* blank.

There's something pinned up, just by the door.

I move closer to it, and see it's very like a reward

chart – the sort Dot has. (I MUST NOT HIDE HAM UNDER MY PILLOW FOR ALASTAIR; I MUST BRUSH ALL MY TEETH; and, of course, I MUST NOT PUT GLITTER IN THE SHAMPOO BOTTLE.)

On this chart, though, Sunshine, Kitt and Pearl's names are in the down column, with a bunch of unconnected words and letters along the top. At a quick glance I make out stuff like SPRING, V.S., M.R. and CATCH. What's that all about? In the grid underneath are a series of ticks and crosses. Most of the crosses are under Pearl's name, I can't help but notice, and a few are under Sunshine's. Kitt's boxes seem cross-free . . .

'What's this?' I ask, without thinking that it might be a nosy question.

'It's just our training – oh!'

Pearl slaps her hand over her mouth as Kitt appears in the bedroom doorway.

'Your sister is shouting for you, Riley,' says Kitt, her lips tight and her eyes the dark brooding grey of stormclouds.

I don't need telling twice; I'm out of there quicker than Kitt's eyes can change colour. 'Bye,' I mumble to Sunshine and Pearl.

'Oh, and happy birthday for tomorrow, Riley!' Sunshine calls after me.

It would be a nice thing to say, if it didn't remind me of the stupid school trip to Wildwoods Theme Park, and if it didn't give me the shivers, since I can't remember telling her about my birthday.

And then I feel *another* shiver as I hear a snatch of conversation drift down behind me.

'*Please*, Kitt, not another black cross for me and Sunshine?' I hear Pearl groan as I pitter-patter down the stairs.

It's my third day of knowing Sunshine, Kitt and Pearl, and I think I understand them *less* than the moment we first met, if that's possible.

Get me out of here, *now* . . .

The opposite of wonderful

I'm in shock.

Something unexpected has happened.

I woke up a minute ago and realized I felt funny.

I felt . . . *happy*.

Happy birthday to me!

And here's what's making me unusually, deliciously happy this particular morning: I'm lying stretched out in my bed, with the sun glowing through the curtains as if it's mid-summer and not mid-autumn. And, ridiculously, my head feels floaty-light, like it's – like it's *stuffed* full of birthday balloons.

Ha!

Riley Roberts, for your twelfth birthday, you have gone slightly insane, but in a good way, so who cares? I laugh to myself.

And since my birthday is a day that links us more than any other, I have a sudden urge to see Mum's smiling face. I didn't get round to framing her photo last night, because I spotted a scratch on the glass as well as the dent to the tatty white frame and thought she deserved better than that.

But, just as I push myself up on to my elbow and lean over to open the knicker drawer, my door is slammed open by a large rabbit.

'HAPPY BIRTHDAY TO YOU!' shrieks Dot. 'SQUASHED TOMATOES AND STEW!!'

She bounces herself on to the bed with such force that the floppy-eared hood of her onesie flies off.

'OK! Thanks!' I say, trying to stop myself being smothered with love and fleecy material.

'You have to come downstairs NOW!' she

demands, hopping off me and grabbing my hand in her paw.

'Can't I just wake up first?' I ask, but rabbits don't seem to take no for an answer, and I let myself be dragged downstairs, half-awake and yawning.

'Happy birthday!' three voices sing out as I'm shoved into the living room.

No – there's something wrong here.

The bunny didn't join in.

And there's only Dad and Hazel standing here in the room.

Yet I'm *sure* I heard a third voice.

'Riley! Oi!'

My heart skips a beat as I recognize that third voice and hear it clearly again, from the computer on the desk in the alcove.

The desk looks like a shrine: all birthday cake and candles and presents . . . and a smiling face beaming at me on the screen.

Behind her is the glow of a pinky-orange evening

sky and lazily drooping palm fronds. They're twelve or so hours ahead of us, so it's been my birthday in New Zealand for practically a whole day already.

'Tia!' I gasp, perching myself on the chair in front of the screen. With her golden-brown skin and acid-lime vest top, she looks bright-eyed and beautiful – and there I am in the corner of the screen, all sleepy morning face and my crummy old spotty PJs.

But for once I don't care how scuzzy I look; those imaginary birthday balloons in my head are making me feel deliciously giddy and giggly.

The last few weeks I've expected my birthday to be the pits, but it might turn out to be a little bit wonderful after all . . .

Who was I kidding?

After the thrill of seeing Tia, of buzzing at the idea that she'd planned my birthday Skype surprise with Dad before she left, of opening my presents (a proper grown-up compact camera from Dad and

Hazel, a locket with our photos in from Tia), *everything* went the opposite of wonderful.

POP! went the first of my imaginary balloons when I realized how late Tia's call had made me, and I got a telling off from Mrs Mahoney for being last on the waiting coach outside the school gates.

POP! Another balloon burst when I found the only free seat left on the coach was next to Mr Thomlinson. I mean, what do you talk to a deputy head about? With my tummy tied in nervous knots, I spotted my get-out a couple of minutes into our journey: as Mr Thomlinson leaned across the aisle to chat with Mrs Mahoney, I pretended to fall asleep – for the *whole* of the two-hour trip to Wildwoods Theme Park.

Once we'd arrived and got the lecture from Mr Thomlinson about appropriate behaviour, and threats of certain death (sort of) if we weren't back at the coach by three o'clock, I slunk off alone into the teeming crowds, staring after the gangs of boisterous boys and the arm-linking groups of girls, all laughing and hurrying towards the rides. Sunshine, Kitt and Pearl . . . I hadn't a clue where *they'd* got to. But, hey, I didn't have a clue about them a lot of the time . . .

'You look deep in thought, Riley!' a familiar voice says now.

I turn and smile at Mrs Mahoney, hoping she doesn't ask what exactly I've been thinking. Cos for the last few hours, as I've wandered around unseen and unnoticed by all the other Hillcrest Year 7s, I've been thinking that today – actually this whole *week* – has been like a ride on one of these roller-coasters.

Up, down, back and forth.

Up, up, *up* I've gone, loving seeing Tia's old room, like it's hovering in the sky; loving hearing my photos being praised at school; loving my birthday message from my distant but still best friend.

Down, down, *down* I've plunged, missing Tia; being made a fool of by Lauren; spending my birthday with no one.

Back and forth I've lurched, meeting my new neighbours; trying to decide whether they like me or not; trying to figure out if the jumble and tumble of assorted weirdnesses that've been happening means there's something really, really *strange* going on in my world or if I'm just so frazzled with loneliness that my over-active imagination is frying my brain . . .

'So which rides have you been on so far?' asks Mrs Mahoney, realizing I'm not going to answer her first question.

'Um, none,' I admit, then when I see her stunned expression I quickly show her the viewer on my camera. 'But see – I've been wandering around taking pictures of everyone having fun!'

It's lame, I know, but I don't want Mrs Mahoney guessing that I'm a pathetic friend-free zone, or she might do that primary-school trick of taking the little kid's hand and asking a bunch of reluctant schoolmates if they'll play nicely with you.

And, anyway, it's been kind of interesting taking

those photos. I noticed a couple of the girls had ditched their regulation ironed long-haired look and were wearing cute plaits. Ellie Stevens from Woody's class had crimped her hair, and the crinkly waves really suit her. A girl whose name I don't know from Y7E had even tied her hair into two tight little top-knots. And out of school uniform there seemed to be so many different colours of hoodies and skinny jeans; there was hardly any grey or black to be seen.

'Ooh, these look super!' says Mrs Mahoney, flipping through snap after snap of Hillcrest students queuing, laughing, shrieking and screaming.

There's one of Woody and his mates on the Red River Canyon ride (they'll be soggy on the way home) and a bunch of girls in my class whirling above my head – arms and legs dangling like ragdolls – on the bat-tastic hanging roller-coaster.

I've spotted Lauren and her mates from time to time, but haven't wasted a shot on them.

I haven't seen Sunshine, Kitt and Pearl at *all*.

Maybe they're staying out of my way, taking offence at being told by Hazel this morning to make their own way to school, since I was busy opening my presents.

'But, wait, did I hear right? You haven't been on any rides *at all*?' Mrs Mahoney repeats incredulously. 'Riley, it's nearly time to get the coach back! Come on ... let's quickly find you something to go on.'

No! It's my worst little-kid nightmare: Mrs Mahoney has taken me by the hand, and seems to be dragging me over towards the Haunted House.

'Ah – now *there* are some of your classmates, right near the front of the queue! 'Scuse me! Thank you! Sorry, but can this girl squeeze by and join her friends? They're keeping her place for her!' Mrs Mahoney white-lies to the shuffling strangers in the queue as we duck and dive under the barriers.

Finally, she passes me over to the 'care' of three girls I would never in a million years describe as my friends.

'Lauren!' Mrs Mahoney says with a big, beaming, clueless smile. 'Can you girls do me a favour and take Riley on this ride with you? She hasn't been on a single one all day, can you believe tha– Uh-oh, what are those silly boys up to . . .?'

As Mrs Mahoney bobs her way back under barriers to split up a spat between some Hillcrest boys, I find myself being stared at and smirked at, and I don't know which feels worse.

POP! goes another of my imaginary balloons.

'Did I just *hear* that? You haven't been on *anything*?' Lauren spits out, as if she's been told I like to wash my hair in camel wee or something equally gross.

'Hey,' mutters Joelle, holding her hand up to her mouth as if that would stop me from hearing whatever poisonous whisperings she's going to come out with. 'Check out the badge!'

'Oh, yeah!' giggles Nancy from behind her chipped black fingernails.

'What is it?' says Lauren, frowning and unceremoniously flicking the badge I forgot that

I'm wearing. The badge that came with Dad and Hazel's card. ' "KEEP CALM IT'S YOUR BIRTHDAY!"'? OMG, that is *so* tragic!!'

POP!

Lauren's acid words burn straight through the rubber of *that* imaginary balloon.

Her fingers fly away from my badge as if it's toxic, as if *I'm* toxic. And with that one casually cruel small gesture, before I know it, this whole rotten roller-coaster of a day catches up with me.

'Hey, look – now she's crying!' I hear Joelle titter.

'What's up, Riley?' Lauren calls out. 'Is you a ickle bit scared of the nasty Haunted House?'

Joelle and Nancy double up, cackling at the cartoon kiddie voice she's just put on.

POP! POP! Two *more* of my birthday balloons of happiness vanish.

'Do it again!' giggles Joelle, egging her friend on.

Lauren seems happy to oblige. 'Is ickle Riley a bit fwightened of the scary ride?' she mocks me. 'Not got Tia to hold your hand any more?'

POP! POP! POP!

Lauren tosses back her hair, enjoying herself immensely. 'Or does Riley need a cuddle from her mumsy-wumsy maybe?' she adds, unaware that her throwaway remark is like a punch to my chest.

POP! POP! POP! POP! go my final happiness balloons.

An overwhelming sense of panic rushes through me and I feel utterly naked without Tia. Lauren wouldn't have talked to me like this with her by my side. Cool, confident Tia was a don't-mess forcefield, and suddenly I'm just this vulnerable, pathetic recipe for Awkward Shy Jelly, which Lauren is more than happy to squish.

I'm so alone, I realize with a crush of my heart, and a thud of a stray elbow as a couple of boys who were standing directly behind us jostle me aside, now that one of the Haunted House attendants has called for two people to come forward to fill a car.

'Can I ask you a question, Lauren?' a brusque voice suddenly asks.

Who said that? Was it *Kitt*?

Through my blur of tears I turn and see a cute pair of dark 'ears', a waterfall of gold-red hair, the bright white of stubby plaits.

Sunshine, Kitt and Pearl; I hadn't spotted them before – those boys and my panic had blinded me to their presence.

'What sort of question?' Lauren snips, squaring up to Kitt.

Blinking my tears away, I focus on my next-door neighbours. Kitt is the sternest I've ever seen her, though luckily it's not *me* she's glowering at through her intense black glasses.

But Sunshine and Pearl – they look worried. In fact, Sunshine is saying something, talking in words no one can hear. But I think – I *think* I just lip-read what they were . . . 'Kitt – *don't! Remember the rules!*'

Suddenly something occurs to me.

Kitt's dagger eyes.

Her tight-lipped, stony face.

Maybe she has anger issues and is meant to be controlling them.

The chart on the wall of the loft, did Mr and Mrs Angelo put it up there? Do all those strange words and initials refer to 'good' behaviours the girls are working on?

'Do you *like* being mean?' Kitt now asks Lauren. 'Does it feel good?'

If Lauren was a cat, her ears would be flat on her head right now, getting ready to lash out and –

'OK, *HOW* MANY PEOPLE?' the Haunted House attendant accidentally interrupts with a bellow as we all suddenly find ourselves next in line.

'Three!' Joelle says quickly, and, before I know it, she, Nancy and Lauren are ushered into a slowly trundling, morbidly decorated carriage.

Yay! I *don't* have to sit with them, despite Mrs Mahoney's best efforts.

'AND YOU – HOW MANY PEOPLE?' the attendant now barks at me.

No! Is this *the* moment I was dreading all week? The moment everyone sees me slouch on to a ride *on my own*?

'Four,' says Sunshine, ushering me into the front of the bat-covered car while she slips into the seat behind.

'RIGHT, QUICK AS YOU CAN!' says the attendant as Kitt slides on to the red-plastic banquette beside me and Pearl bobs down next to Sunshine.

Clunk! Clunk! go the barriers over our laps, locking me and Kitt and Sunshine and Pearl in pairs.

With a rattle and lurch of metal, our car and the one in front trundle forward along the tracks towards the dark swing doors that will lead us into the Haunted House.

Just as the front car pushes those doors open I see three faces turn to smirk at us, each as witchy as anything that's probably inside. Joelle and Nancy are grinning at some viperish words spilling out of Lauren's mouth, words I can't make out.

OK, maybe only *I* can't make them out.

'Kitt,' says Sunshine in what sounds like a warning voice, placing her hand on her sister's shoulder.

Kitt gives a little twitch beside me, and glowers as the car in front of us lurches off into the tunnel with a thwack of doors and a demonic screech.

Now it's our turn, and the car hurtles us forward into a pit of darkness with the deafening noise of screams, bells, roars and blood-curdling groans of agony.

But despite the gloom and the racket the ride's a bit feeble really – no more scary than the kids who turn up at the door at Halloween. I mean, even in the gloom you can see that every looming neon skeleton, every gurning skull, every draping cobweb, every coffin, vampire, ghost and ghoulie looks a bit tatty and unconvincing.

Even though I'm being wobbled around, I grab my new camera out of my bag, thinking that I may as well take a few snaps to show Dot, since it's more likely to give her a fit of giggles than a case of night terrors.

With my viewfinder, I focus on Kitt beside me – and see that her face is rigid.

Whoa . . . is she scared?

Or am *I* scared suddenly?

Her eyes in the darkness are glowing *silver white*.

Wait – maybe it's a version of red-eye. Maybe I just need to read the instructions for my new camera later and find a button to switch off so it won't –

WHOOSHHHH!

A momentary, *intense* glow of light fills the entire tunnel, so bright it practically X-rays my hands where they're clutching the camera.

It's such an impressive special effect that I take everything back that I said about the ride being useless.

'EEEEEEEEEEEEEEEEEEEEEEEKKKKK! AAARGGHHHHHHH!!!'

And that scream – it's so real and heartfelt it sends shivers down my spine.

Thwack!!

We're through the exit doors and out into the dazzle of daylight, the ride over. Except it's not, for someone.

'*AAARGGHHHHHHHHHHHHHHHHH!!!*' The screaming continues, even though the cars have clunked to a standstill, and the theme-park staff are ushering us off.

'GET IT OFF ME *NOOOOWWWWW*!' shrieks a voice that is unmistakably Lauren's.

I bound out of the car and try to see what's going on.

Oh, there . . . by the COME BACK AND VISIT US AGAIN SOO-OOO-OON sign. Boys are laughing and pointing as Joelle and Nancy desperately tear at something that looks suspiciously like giant cobwebs, which cling to Lauren's head and shoulders.

She's like a demented Bride of Dracula and sounds like one too.

'AND THE SPIDERS! THE *SPIDERS*!' Lauren shrieks again as scrabbling black specks hurtle down her face, neck and arms.

'Chill out, Lauren!' laughs a boy I recognize as Woody. 'They're only made of plastic!'

It must be an optical illusion. The toy insects really *do* look as if they're moving – till they drop off with a plastic plink on to the ground and lie lifeless.

Click! snaps my camera, capturing the surreal moment.

'It's like half the Haunted House props collapsed on Lauren while she was in there!' I say, turning to the others and catching Sunshine mouthing something silently at Kitt: *You shouldn't have done that.*

Kitt silently mouths something back: *I know, I know – sorry.*

Prickles and tickles – the hairs on my arms stand up as a shocking idea bursts into my head, like a firework set off too close for comfort.

Was that weirdness in the Haunted House somehow down to *Kitt* – and because of *me*?

And it's not just the last few minutes on the ride that's getting to me.

I mean, *everything* that's happened over the last

few days, it isn't just coincidence after coincidence, is it?

I might have a talent for imagining things, but all the surprising, confusing, unbelievable moments this last week . . . could they be for *real*?

Most importantly, does it all have something to do with these sisters?

'Sunshine?' Pearl says out loud, pointing at me. 'Should we . . .'

Sunshine and Kitt seem to shake themselves and remember I'm standing here. The clouds lift from Sunshine's face and she instantly radiates a smile that could chase all your worries away. Nearly.

'Riley,' she says in her silky soft, calming voice, oblivious to Lauren still screeching and stamping in the background. 'We have a present for you.'

Sunshine rummages in her bag and gently pulls out a flat rectangular parcel wrapped in white tissue and blue ribbon.

I feel instantly guilty, like I've been caught thinking treasonous thoughts.

Without making eye contact, I take the parcel Sunshine is holding out and tentatively pull at the bow.

Peeling the rustling paper back, I find myself holding a mirror-edged photo frame, delicately engraved with meandering swirls. Reflected in the silvered surround is the blue sky above us, dazzling my eyes.

'It's for a special photo,' says Sunshine.

Wow, another coincidence.

Another strange and wonderful coincidence and it's taken my breath away.

Though, like I say, I'm not sure I believe in those any more . . .

'Do you *have* a special photo?' Pearl asks, blinking hopefully at me.

'I have the perfect one,' I answer with a slightly croaky voice.

I'm picturing another image of blue sky: Mum on Folly Hill with arms flung wide and carefree, me curled up safe inside her.

It's perfect.

It's the most *perfect* present, better than . . . well, *all* the others I've had, lovely as they are.

'Riley, are you *crying*?' asks Sunshine, tilting her head in concern when she spots my tears. She and her sisters are staring at me like explorers who've discovered a new species of butterfly.

'Oh!' gasps Pearl. 'We thought you'd be pleased!'

'I am,' I laugh. 'These are happy tears!'

I rummage in my pocket, searching for a tissue I'm pretty sure is in there.

They've given me a present . . . does this mean they absolutely, really, truly do like me? And am I ready to absolutely, really, truly trust these strange and special girls?

'Riley?'

'Yes?' I say, glancing up at Pearl.

'Don't you want to get that?'

Pearl, smiling broadly at me, nods at my bag at the very *second* the trill of a text message pings through.

With a slightly trembling hand, I go to pick up the phone.

The Haunted House didn't spook me, but my new sort-of-friends sort of do . . .

With a rustle and a flutter

My eyes are squeezed tight shut.

So tight I can see spangles of bright light dancing against the darkness of my eyelids.

I'm straining to make out her voice, telling me that everything will be all right.

And I *can* hear a voice, only it's not my mum's.

'Um, please don't do that. If you scrunch your face that way, I can't put your mascara on.'

I blink my eyes open.

The make-up girl is looming over me, her expression slightly weary.

No wonder – the noise is unbearable.

The rest of Year 7 went home as soon as the coaches dropped us back from Wildwoods Theme Park, but all of Y7C is here, packed into the library, gossiping and yakking and waiting for the crew from the local TV station to finish faffing around with sound-checks and lighting and mascara-ing and get on with making them all stars. In the background at least.

'I'll have to find some hairspray – I've *got* to do something about hiding that bald spot,' the make-up girl grumbles, going off to rummage in another toolbox of styling products.

'OK, Riley?' asks Mrs Sharma.

She's sitting on the stool next to me, her make-up already done, her baby sleeping peacefully in her arms.

'I don't think I can do this,' I tell her, my stomach in knots of worry.

'Riley, I only just came out of hospital a few hours ago, and *I'm* doing it,' she says.

'But it's *your* story,' I point out.

'*And* yours,' Mrs Sharma says firmly.

It's OK for Mrs Sharma – she's confident and pretty, and will be able to look into the lens of a camera and smile and chat.

Ever since I got the text from Mr Thomlinson – just after we'd stepped off the Haunted House ride – I've felt sick, having found out that the local TV channel want to interview Mrs Sharma and me about her novelty birth for this evening's news.

They'd picked up the story from the newspaper – the piece done in the hospital, of course. And, unknown to me, while I'd been mooching around Wildwoods, the TV people had arranged it all with my form teacher, my head, my dad even.

And so here I am, in complete shock, with a bald spot that'll show up under the spotlight, and with no Tia to tell me it'll be OK.

I can't even turn to my are-they-aren't-they friends, Sunshine, Kitt and Pearl.

At the theme park, by the time Mr Thomlinson had told me what was awaiting me back at school, everyone had already filed on to the waiting coach. Once I finally climbed aboard, I'd spotted Sunshine, Kitt and Pearl fast asleep together on the back seat – Kitt paper-pale in the middle with her foster sisters either side, protective arms wrapped round her. There was no space beside them – I ended up at the front again, stuck beside Mrs Mahoney this time.

So I didn't have the girls' company on the way home, and I haven't caught sight of them since we arrived here.

Maybe they've gone home already?

After all, Kitt didn't look too well after what happened – whatever that was – during the Haunted House ride . . .

'I really can't go out there, in front of the cameras,' I mutter again, lost in the grip of fear and loneliness, with no one to help make me brave.

'Come on, Riley – look at yourself! Look how you stand out!' says Mrs Sharma, pointing across the room at the row of self-portraits on the wall. 'Now do it in real life!'

OK, so my stark black-and-white photo *does* actually look quite good now I think about it, but that's only because Tia's has faded even more with the sunlight coming through the window, and Lauren's has peeled off the wall altogether. (She was still peeling off cobwebs and raging all the way home on the coach.)

'It's all right, I suppose,' I admit. 'But it's not as good as Tia's.'

'Actually, Riley ... now you've mentioned her, I've been meaning to say something,' Mrs Sharma says more gently. 'You know, I think that perhaps Tia leaving might be good for you, in a way. I think on your own, you'll blossom!'

Blossom?

Tia going to New Zealand is something I should be *pleased* about?

All my fondness for Mrs Sharma evaporates in a nanosecond.

How can she say something like that about my best friend, about the only person who ever stood up for me, who was ever on my side?

As the make-up girl comes back over, now armed with mega-hold hairspray, I have an urge to escape.

'Got to go to the loo,' I say, slipping off my stool and hurrying away.

'Riley!' Mrs Sharma's voice trails behind.

'Riley!' a boy's voice says close by. 'I was telling the director guy about your photos.'

It's Woody, all gangly and grinning, some dark spikes of hair falling over his brown eyes. Why is he blocking my way? Why is he holding up my holiday project? What's he even doing here? He's not in my class; he wasn't part of what happened on Monday morning in the gym when Mrs Sharma went into labour. It was only Y7C that was asked to stay behind when the coach dropped us off here.

'Anyway,' he carries on, ignoring my confused expression, 'the director asked me to stick this up

201

on the wall where Lauren's picture was, right next to your self-portrait, and he's going to position you and Mrs Sharma there for the filming. Isn't that cool?'

Huh? I don't know why Woody's acting like he's my agent or something. OK, so it's kind of him, but I'm *way* too frazzled to have this conversation; instead I bolt out of the library with a thud of swinging doors and hurry along the long cream corridor before anyone can stop me.

Happy birthday to me? I think as my head, heart and footsteps thunder. *Ha! I just want to get off this roller-coaster of a day . . .*

Suddenly, my thundering steps turn to pitter-pats as I begin to slow down and stare at the glints on the ground. Flickers of glitter – silver glitter – lead to the girls' loos on the left.

(*A sudden memory: Folly Hill, Tia telling me her news, the sense of glitter sprinkling on my face . . .*)

Softly, without creating a creak, I push the door open and peek inside. And it seems as if I've walked in on an argument. Even if it does happen to be a silent one.

Sunshine's normally calm face is a picture of anger, her finger wagging in Kitt's face, her pretty lips moving fast and furious.

Kitt looks worn out, her head hung low, leaning back against a sink.

Pearl is on the other side of Kitt – a hand on the mirrored glass above the row of sinks – watching, listening and worrying, by the look on her delicate face.

'Everything all right?' I ask, wary of invading the space of these unknowable girls.

'Yes,' Sunshine says briskly, ditching her anger and her wagging finger and adopting an instant expression of serenity.

'It's fine,' Pearl adds, dropping her hand and straightening up as she sees me.

Kitt says nothing, her eyes ringed with the bruised colour of exhaustion, but that's not what's made me jerk in surprise. It's the silver fingerprints on the mirror, right where Pearl was resting her hand.

(*Silver fingerprints on my front door the morning I waved Tia away, like some strange foretelling of things to come . . .*)

'Everything is . . . good!' says Sunshine, her voice cracking a little as if she's not quite telling the truth.

(*Silver waves of glitter trailing along my garden fence . . . silver glitter on the cuff of my sleeve where Pearl touched it after Kitt stopped me from stepping in front of that car . . .*)

Now I stare at Pearl, and see something that isn't real.

Because I'm the girl who's good at imagining things.

Because what's peeking up behind her can't be there.

Because a hump of white feathers is rising above her left shoulder, and that's just not possible, is it?

(*A single white feather fluttering on to my keyboard . . .*)

My first instinct is to scream, to turn and run.

But I'm frozen to the spot, statue still.

These girls who've intrigued and confused and sometimes *frightened* me, I somehow feel flooded with the knowledge that they'd never hurt me.

Maybe that's because – in the shocked silence of the moment – I can hear her voice far, far away, like a whisper on the wind, telling me, '*It's going to be all right, Riley . . .*'

And a girl should always listen to her mum, shouldn't she?

With a trembling hand, I reach out towards Pearl.

Kitt suddenly sees what I see and thrusts her own hand out, trying to force whatever it is down, but that's not going to work.

'Riley!' Sunshine says insistently, stepping in front of the girls to hide my view.

Her petrol-tinted eyes as she gazes down at me, the irises seem to be moving swirls of deep blue, purple and green . . . swirls that are almost hypnotizing to watch.

But I'm *not* watching, because, with a rustle and a flutter, two beautiful white feathery wings are

205

unfurling behind Pearl, their tips practically touching the ceiling of the girls' loos.

'Sorry!' Pearl says in her little-girl voice. 'I just couldn't stop it!'

Sunshine closes her eyes and sighs.

It's not the *only* sound; with another rustle and flutter and slight creak, a second pair of wings appear.

'Kitt! Not you too!' Sunshine positively groans, slapping her porcelain hands over her face.

'I can't help it, Sunshine. I'm tired after all the errant magic,' says Kitt.

Errant magic? I mutter in my head, wondering what that is, though it seems almost unimportant considering what I'm currently staring at open-mouthed.

'Which you *shouldn't* have done,' Sunshine says flatly, her face still covered. 'Everything was going really well without you breaking the rules, Kitt.'

'Yes, *I* know,' grumbles Kitt. '*Don't lose your temper. Don't seek revenge, for yourself or for others.*'

'Or Riley!' Pearl pipes up.

(*Revenge? Has that got something to do with Lauren? With cobwebs and spiders and blasts of silver-white light . . .?*)

'*You* can talk!' Kitt turns and says spikily to her sister. 'I've had to cover for you breaking the rules *loads* of times, Pearl! *And* you, Sunshine. You kept letting your thoughts be heard! I had to watch the two of you *all* the time!'

So *that's* why Kitt didn't encourage our friendship. She was busy protecting Sunshine and Pearl, *not* hating me.

But these rules they're talking about . . . Is it something to do with that chart I saw on the wall of their bedroom?

'Sunshine,' I whisper, hoping the most straightforward of the Angelos can help me make sense of what's happening before my head explodes with shock. 'What . . . what does it all mean?'

At my words Sunshine slowly drops her hands.

Her face lifts.

And, as her eyes open, a silver-white beam of light

spills from them, illuminating the whole space with breath-taking brightness.

(*The unearthly glow of light from Tia's house when I was up on Folly Hill with Dad . . .*)

With an immense rush and crackle of unfurling, Sunshine's own wings reach up, up, up towards the ceiling.

Kitt and Pearl slip either side of her, their own eyes blazing with matching light, Pearl's giddiness and Kitt's exhaustion gone for the moment as they stand sentry to their sister.

'Riley, do you know what we are?' asks Sunshine as Kitt and Pearl mouth those same words.

The room – the stupid, ordinary tiled room – feels like it's vibrating.

The sensation is rising through my feet, gentle tremors travelling up my body, making the hairs on my arms prickle and tickle.

(*Prickles and tickles . . . like feathers stroking my skin . . .*)

'Wow, Dot and Coco were right, weren't they?' I

murmur to myself. Angels really *had* moved in next door to us.

'I-I *knew* there was something special about you . . . I just didn't think you'd b-be what you *are*,' I stumble and stutter, not managing to say the amazing 'angel' word, as if it was too magical to say out loud. 'But, but why are you here? Living in my road? Going to my school?'

The intensity of the light suddenly fades, so I can look into the girls' now steely-silver eyes without wincing.

'We're here to help,' Sunshine says, her wings rippling behind her.

'Who?' I ask.

Sunshine puts her hands on my shoulders and turns me to the long mirror above the sinks. 'You,' she replies as all three girls stare fondly at me.

'Me?' I croak.

'We're here to look for humans who've stopped shining. Well, we're learning to,' Kitt explains, her energy leaving her and her wings trembling as she leans on the nearest porcelain sink. 'You're our first.'

Me.

So basically I'm a test case for trainee angels?

'Hold on, I've stopped "shining"? What does that mean?' I ask in a panic. 'Am I dying?'

'No, you're not dying, Riley!' Sunshine assures me. 'But if a human's shine fades altogether it can never come back, and it can leave you with sadness for all of your life.'

'We sensed you fading,' says Kitt, who seems to be fading herself. 'Your shine was already weakened, because of what happened to your mother.'

'You know . . .?' I murmur.

'Yes, but that wasn't the main reason for fading,' says Pearl, curling an arm round mine. 'It was because of your friend.'

'Tia leaving?' I say, still barely breathing, barely believing what I'm seeing.

'Yes, but it had begun to happen before that,' Sunshine says, gazing at me sympathetically in the mirror.

Before that? What do they mean, *before* that?

'Look, listen . . .' Sunshine whispers, taking my hot hand in her cool palm, Pearl wrapping icy fingers round my other hand, Kitt resting her head on Pearl's fragile shoulder.

Like a hiss on a wire, I hear it; I see it.

Tia talking, me listening.

Tia joking, me laughing.

Tia in technicolour, me in black and white.

Tia being wonderful, smart, beautiful; me being ordinary, ordinary, ordinary.

It wasn't her fault.

It was *mine*.

Like Woody, I was in awe of Tia. And as we'd got older, especially since we'd started at bustling, busy Hillcrest Academy, I'd allowed myself to hide more and more in her shadow, to become more and more invisible.

A few minutes ago I'd been mad at Mrs Sharma, but maybe she was right.

Tia *was* fun and *was* my friend, but our super-strong bond was suffocating me. And maybe her too . . .

SLAM!!

'Riley!' bellows Lauren, crashing through the door. 'Are you in heeeee—'

She freezes.

Only her long blonde hair sways slightly as she comes to a halt.

I think for a second it's the shock of seeing three angels in the first-floor girls' toilets, till I notice Sunshine, Kitt and Pearl's steady stare.

Lauren – she's as still as the statue staring out over Folly Hill.

I'm suddenly a little scared for her. 'What are you doing?' I ask, uncertain whether I should stand beside Lauren in case she falls. 'Are you hypnotizing her? Don't hurt her!'

The girls – the *angels* – step closer and closer to

Lauren. I might not feel like they mean *me* any harm, but Lauren hasn't exactly shown her best side to them. If she's actually got one, of course.

'We're rewinding . . .' Sunshine says in a soft, otherworldly voice.

Uh-oh. What does that mean?

'Open the door, Riley,' says Kitt, locked into the sisters' mutual moment of concentration.

I get behind the rigid form of Lauren and yank the door open.

'Help her walk backwards,' Pearl instructs me.

Touching the arm of the girl who's hurt me so much, I guide her – in a trance – out of the room, into the cool cream-coloured corridor and leave her there.

I return to the loos and close the door to the sound of crackles and ruffles.

'She won't remember anything,' says Sunshine as the silver light fades to blue, the wings folding and melding back out of sight.

(*Mr Angelo nearly falling from the tree, then looking only*

213

slightly baffled at losing his hammer – he could remember nothing . . .)

Under the plain glare of the ceiling spotlights Pearl looks girlish and wide-eyed again; Kitt is once again stumbling and bone-tired.

'When Lauren comes in here, you have to go out, Riley,' Sunshine continues, telling me, rather than asking me. 'You have to be with Mrs Sharma in front of everyone, to help strengthen your shine.'

The anxiety clutches at my chest again.

'Please don't make me,' I beg. 'It's all – it's all too much. This . . . and, well, *everything.*'

'It's going to be all right, Riley,' Sunshine beams at me, using words that chime in my heart. 'You *can* do this on your own, because we've been working with you, even though you haven't known it.'

(Mum's voice telling me everything would be all right; was that the girls too . . .?)

'Riley, I think I can do one more thing to make you feel better,' Kitt says, interrupting my thoughts and stepping closer to me, looking so tired

I wouldn't be surprised if she climbed on to the shelf that ran under the wall-length mirrors and fell asleep.

'*No*,' Sunshine says sternly. 'There've been enough black crosses. And look at you, Kitt! You've used all your energies today!'

But Kitt isn't listening; Kitt is placing her hands on my head, and it's as if warm water is cascading through my hair.

'Riley!' bellows Lauren, crashing through the door – *again*. 'Are you in here . . .? OMG, what's going on?'

Like a tap being turned off, the warm sensation instantly disappears.

'Are you OK?' I ask, catching Kitt as she stumbles.

'Just go,' she whispers.

I hesitate, but see she has two people who love her, who'll help her.

'What's wrong with *her*?' Lauren snarls, pointing her finger at Kitt.

'She's allergic to you – same as the rest of us,' I say as I slip past her in the doorway.

Steering myself back to the library and the waiting TV crew, I buzz inside, feeling that my skin is just a little bit thicker, and that I won't let Lauren, or people like her, hurt me the same way ever again.

Cos it's time to stop worrying about being just me.

Time to stop hiding behind the bright star that was Tia.

Time to start shining for myself . . .

After everything changed ...

I have the *strangest* feeling.

If I was at home I'd think Dot was standing over me, trying not to giggle while she sprinkled glitter on my face, after telling me to lie down and shut my eyes.

But I'm not at home.

Right now I'm in my favourite place with my favourite people: Sunshine, Kitt and Pearl.

We're doing what we do best.

Lying on our backs at the top of Folly Hill, right by the Angel.

We can't feel the soft green grass on our bare legs and arms, because we're bundled up in our cosy parkas, coats and duffels, stretched out on the tartan blanket I borrowed from Alastair's doggy basket. But we are staring up at the unusually blue November sky and the skimming white clouds that promise rain later.

Me, Sunshine, Kitt and Pearl.

Talking about everything.

Talking about nothing.

Talking about balloons . . .

'Did you like them?' Pearl asks hopefully.

'You mean you *put* them in my head?' I say, surprised.

That sense of happiness on the morning of my twelfth birthday, like my brain was full of balloons; Pearl's only *just* remembered to tell me it was a special birthday present from her.

'I hope I didn't put too many in there,' she says, biting her lip. 'I worried I'd make you dizzy!'

Finding out about what the angels have done and can do . . . It'll take time to know it all, but I don't mind waiting.

In the meantime I should ask them about this feeling of glitter sprinkling on to my face.

'Look! LOOK, RILEY! It's like SNOW!' shrieks Dot, and I open my eyes to see that my sort-of-stepsister is dropping blades of grass – white-tipped with frost – down on to me.

'Dot!' I yelp, sitting up and brushing the blades away. 'Haven't you got a dog to play with?'

'TWO of them!' she giggles, spinning off across the hill, her arms like the rotors of a helicopter.

Irritating as she can be, Dot's great to photograph, and so I pick up my new camera and *click, click, click*. I capture Dot's spin, and Bee and Alastair's romping, Bee gripping the dog lead in his mouth and dragging his wood-pup buddy along with him wherever he goes.

Actually, one recent-ish photo of mine has been a big hit at school – it was blown up huge on the *News Matters* website. It was the moment just after the TV interview last week, when Mrs Sharma was struggling to hold her baby and untangle the tiny

microphone from her top. She'd glanced around for the nearest pair of capable arms, but not finding any (ha!), she plonked her tiny-person-sized parcel on to a startled Woody.

The baby immediately started wailing, and Woody jokingly pretended to wail too. That's the shot I took, and it still makes me laugh now. It made the editorial team at *News Matters* laugh as well, and so they offered me the job of being their site photographer. Funnily enough, around the time I said a shy yes please to that, Lauren Mayhew let the team know she wasn't interested in being a reporter for them any more.

She's told some of the girls in class that it was because it's just not cool enough for her, but I think everyone knows it's got more to do with Mr Thomlinson showing the photos I took at the theme park as a slide show during assembly, *including* the one of Lauren's temper tantrum under the tangle of cobwebs and spiders. Ever since then she's gone pretty quiet in general, and is blanking *me* in particular, which is just fantastic. I mean, I don't for one minute expect her to stay that way; once she's licked her wounds she and her acid tongue will probably be back, as spiky and dangerous as ever.

But by then I'll be ready: a little braver, a little stronger, a whole lot shinier than I used to be.

'Hey, can you take a photo of the stone lady?' Pearl asks me as she jumps up and wanders over to the Angel on her plinth. 'I like her. She's pretty.'

'She's funny,' says Kitt, jumping to her feet and holding her hands in front of her and doing a simpering impression of the statue.

'Hey, Riley,' I hear Sunshine say, though she's still lying down, her lips not moving.

She likes to play this game, to see if I'll hear.

'What?' I answer out loud, keeping one eye on Dot, who knows nothing about who and what these girls really are.

'Why don't you take a photo of the three of us?' She speaks aloud now too, pushing herself up on to her elbows. 'I mean, *us* with *her*.'

As Sunshine joins her sisters at the plinth, I marvel at what I've seen, felt and learned in the last couple of weeks.

I've learned that brand-new angels need to practise their skills, and I'm happy to be Sunshine, Kitt and Pearl's girl-shaped guinea pig.

I've learned that they can make mistakes: Kitt with her anger, and Pearl with her slip-ups of glitter, of bringing dead flowers back to life with a careless touch of her fingers.

I've learned they can take themselves to the brink of exhaustion with a tricky rewind, like, say, when a foster parent loses his footing on a tree . . .

Actually, I've learned what quite a few of the strange words and letters mean on the chart in the loft room. 'Catch' is my favourite so far: the sense of seeing what's about to happen. Which means I understand now why Kitt knew the car was going to move outside school *and* when the old lady on Folly Hill was going to appear and tell me that magical fact, that I looked so like my mum.

And Sunshine, Kitt and Pearl want to help me find out *more* about Mum.

They say it'll help me shine.

Maybe they can help me find out why it hurts Dad quite so much to talk about her?

'Hey, Riley!' Pearl calls out from her spot by the Angel. 'Do you want to get that first?'

I'm used to this type of small catch now, and grab my phone out of my bag, laughing, just *before* the text pings.

Tia, the name glows luminously on the screen.

'It's OK,' I say, slipping the phone back in my bag. 'I'll get it later.'

Tia is still my friend, and I love hearing from her and seeing her photos on Flickr of her house and garden and kidney-shaped pool, but she's doing her thing and I'm beginning to do mine.

'Come on, then, we're ready!' Kitt grins at me, striking her jokey saintly pose again.

I point my camera at the most unlikely three angels you could ever see: one tall and serene with soft tumbles of gold-red hair and untied ankle boots, one staring at me through her dark-rimmed glasses, her ear-shaped buns as funny as she is stern, one bouncing on the spot in her glittery baseball boots to keep warm.

CLICK!

I'll print this out and put it on my pinboard, beside the photo Mrs Mahoney took of me, Mrs Sharma and little Raina Riley Sharma after our filming (it was a bit cringey to watch on TV that night, but, hey, the world didn't end, no one died).

CLICK! CLICK! CLICK!

I take another few as Dot, Bee and Alastair bounce into view.

CLICK! CLICK! CLICK!

'So?' says Sunshine, drifting towards me with what looks like a smile of amusement twitching at the corners of her mouth.

'Hold on,' I say, flicking the button to view what I've just taken. 'Oh!'

Sunshine places a hand on my arm, and I can

feel the relaxing warmth of it through my parka. (She's working towards doing that without touching, so she can get a star under V. S. – virtual stroking – on the training chart.)

'That's just us, Riley . . .' Sunshine's laugh is like the tinkling of soft bells.

She's laughing because she knew how these photos would turn out.

I'm skimming through image after image, and only seeing three blurs of white light in front of the stone statue on her plinth.

'Yeah, so *now* you know what *real* angels look like!' Kitt says wryly.

I glance at my not-quite-flesh-and-blood friends and realize something.

I don't need to imagine Mum whispering her words of comfort to me any more, because I'm pretty sure everything *will* be all right from now on.

Cos I'm fine being me.

Though I'm never going to be *alone*.

Not when there are angels living next door . . .

Acknowledgements

A bundle of thanks to my focus group of enthusiastic ten-year-old readers, who ate the cake I bribed them with and happily chattered on about potential story ideas. Just want to say sorry, Milly, Freya and Ella, that I couldn't use your ace idea about a boarding school for witches ... it just sounded a *tiny* bit familiar (*cough* ... Harry Potter ... *cough*).

And of course it's been just a little bit wonderful to be working again with the lovely Amanda Punter (like old times!) and the equally lovely Anthea Townsend (like new times!).*

* No cake bribery was required in this instance.

Finally, I'd just like to thank the local garden-centre cafe staff for not laughing and pointing at me as I sat huddled over my laptop at the corner table, muttering dialogue to myself for months on end . . .

How to be an Everyday Angel

The Angelo sisters use their magical abilities to help Riley — but you don't have to be a real angel to help others! Check out these six ideas for how to be an everyday angel . . .

1. Say it, don't think it.

A girl you know has a nice new hairstyle. A boy in class who's usually annoying has done a great drawing. Your best friend was really good fun today and made you smile when you were grumpy. You might fleetingly notice and think about stuff like that, but how about saying something out loud? Come right out with a compliment? Giving someone a bit of praise can boost their self-confidence big time. And make you new friends!

2. 'There, there . . .'

Feeling ill is pants. If your friend is off sick with flu or whatever, be aware that she will be feeling
a) ropey,
b) mopey, and
c) like she's missing out on the fun that you and your other friends are having. So get yourself round to hers after school or at the weekend, armed with chat, chocolate and maybe a favourite magazine. Or, if she's infectious, gather your friends to shout, 'Get well soon!' down the phone to her. That should help her smile through the snot!

3. Be an ace listener.

You can tell something is bothering your friend, but she keeps saying she's 'fine'. Maybe she doesn't want to talk in front of others, so how about arranging to have a little time to chat, just the two of you? You can suggest it face to face, or reach out with a text, or even a note. You might not have all the answers, but having someone to splurge her feelings to might be enough to cheer your friend up.

4. 'If you liked that, you might like this...'

Start a book group. And don't just invite your BFs... ask girls you don't know so well, who you know like reading. You might turn people on to books they wouldn't have ever tried before. And, for people who are a little shy, getting together to talk about books and stories and authors is a great way to be sociable. (Don't forget the biscuits — you ALWAYS need biscuits at a book group!)

5. Make homework not suck.

It's easy to get stuck on homework, especially with creative subjects like writing or projects. But being in a group, bouncing ideas around, can really flick a switch on in your brain!
So suggest get-togethers to help each other out — but lay down the rules too:
1) be nice (no poo-pooing what people say),
2) be encouraging (you'd want the same) and
c) no gossiping (you can save that for later, once the homework is done!).

6. Mad makeover time!

If a friend is feeling a little flat or fed-up, get silly with an over-the-top makeover. Invite her round, blast some music on, and try out a ton of different hairstyles and make-up looks on her. Get her to pose in the mirror, or catwalk up and down the bedroom. It'll be even more fun if you get her to do the same to you!

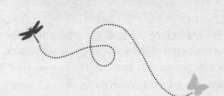

 www.karenmccombie.com

Create a Friendship Collage

A collage that's all about you and your friends —
that's got to look great on your wall, right? Or why don't
you make one in secret, as a surprise for someone?
Of course, there are websites where you can create an
online collage, but there's nothing like getting a bunch of
photos and images and snipping, sticking and gluing
them together by hand!

1. Decide on the theme.

What do you and your friend(s) like to do together? Share a hobby?
Watch movies? What makes you laugh, squeal, drool? Decide on your theme —
and you're ready for Step 2 . . .

2. Grab some photos.

The snaps you use should be of you as well as your friend(s), or group shots
of you together. Choose a variety of sizes and shapes, as well as photos taken
from different times of your life. (If you don't want to use the ACTUAL photos,
copy them on a printer and use the copies instead.)

3. Flick through some mags or the internet.

Browse through magazines or online to select headlines or images
or even just fun words that represent the theme of your collage.
Rip out the pages or print out your favourites to use. You could also look
for a quote from a film or book that you both love, or maybe even
a phrase you always say to each other.

4. Get creative.

For a cool collage, cut each photo into an interesting shape. If you have a photo of you and a friend, for instance, cut round your bodies and discard the background. Or maybe stick your heads on to a star made out of silver foil, or transplant yourselves on to a funny background, like a scene in Harry Potter!

5. Add the words.

The words and phrases you've picked from magazines or online should be a variety of sizes, shapes, fonts and colours.

6. Get gluing!

Stick the larger images on to a poster board (from art shops) or just some cardboard, and then paste other images around them. Try to cover every area of the backing board with either a photo or words. Remember: you can get clever with your background too – if you don't want to have just one big rectangle, you could cut it into a circle, or even a chunky letter from the alphabet, like the first letter of you or your friend's name.

7. Final touches.

Got any tickets from shows you've been to together? Even tickets from things like swimming or ice skating are nice last-minute additions. And scrabble around for some craft stuff to add sparkle, like bits of ribbon or sequins. Even buttons look cute!

8. Tah-nah!

Your collage is ready. Stick it up on your wall, or present it to your friend. And don't forget – you can always update it by adding a new photo to it now and then.

www.karenmccombie.com

Riley's story continues
in . . .

angels
in
training